By: J.K. Rees

PublishAmerica
Baltimore

© 2005 by J. K. Rees.
All rights reserved. No part of this book may be reproduced, stored in a retrieval system or transmitted in any form or by any means without the prior written permission of the publishers, except by a reviewer who may quote brief passages in a review to be printed in a newspaper, magazine or journal.

First printing

At the specific preference of the author, PublishAmerica allowed this work to remain exactly as the author intended, verbatim, without editorial input.

ISBN: 1-4241-0978-7
PUBLISHED BY PUBLISHAMERICA, LLLP
www.publishamerica.com
Baltimore

Printed in the United States of America

I look around this pathetic place and think of the lives these people lead. Am I going crazy, or are these people the drudges of all that is alive in this world as we know it? People are on my nerves so bad anymore that I could destroy them all one at a time. My surroundings are a drunken man sitting to my right, and a woman in her late 20's to my left whom I can only assume is waiting for a date. She seems like the type of woman that has had many experiences like this before. I have never seen her here, which tells me that she is using this place as a neutral ground for a date meet up point.

She sees me smoking a cigarette and asks me for a light. I turn and nod as I light her cigarette and she glances at me and asks my name. I tell her. She introduces herself as Sheila. Sheila then tells me why she is here (as if I care). Her straightforwardness is very awkward, which in return makes me uneasy. I want to get up and scream to her that I don't care, but I listen to it anyway. I realize that I don't have anyway out of this pathetic display of fake kindness on her part, but I don't want to be rude.

Sheila goes on and on for minutes telling me about this guy she is meeting. He's a mutual friend of one of her closest girlfriends and this is their first date. For my own amusement I ask her what she likes in a guy and she is taken back by the question as if I had hit her square in the face. She looks at me as if she didn't give me permission to talk and how dare I interrupt her. I give her a disgusted look as though whatever she has to say I will not be interested in, and I go back to taking a sip from my pint.

I tell Mike the bartender to get me another as I sit and listen to this yippee dog next to me. Doesn't she realize I haven't paid any attention to her for the last few minutes? I look over her shoulder while she is still "blah"-ing at me… and guess who it is? My knight in shining armor! He finally arrives and as quick as she is talking to me she swings herself in his direction and picks up where she left off with me. Whew, I never did think that would end, but it appears to solidify my reason as to why I can't stand people in this world today.

I whisper to the drunken man next to me my sarcastic apologies for the rude behavior I must have displayed when I asked her such a deep and personal question. He just chuckles and says, "It was nothing." I ask drunken man his name and he tells me, "Jim". I turn a little and look up to watch the TV behind the bar, and see that Senator Bowman is now taking a break from this campaign crap for President. I guess I should be a little excited since this is a hometown boy that made it big, but with what I know about that waste of human existence….. I just let it go.

I hate politics and I try not to get so involved with it, but after seeing it every time I turn on the TV, I realize you can't escape it. A big game will be playing and then a news break about a character out of the song 'Cult of Personality' comes on the screen and tells you how things went so well for him today on the campaign trail. Who cares!? I just want to see if the Colts scored! Yes, I am a die hard Colts fan. I always have been since they left Baltimore. What else is there to do here in Indy?

I hate basketball, and never liked that blow hard Bob Knight even though the Hoosier state is known for that orange ball sport. I swear, the closer I get to Bloomington, the more I see the color red and posters of that jerk make me despise him more. I don't know who, or what I hate more: Indiana for making this man a god, or that man for knowing it, and pushing it to the limit to where that school had to fire him.

Anyway, Senator Bowman is a rat, and when people find out about him they will feel the same as I. I look over at Jim and ask him what he thinks about Bowman and he replies, "I don't. I've always hated politics. They're all crooked." Jim and I toast to that as I smile lifting my glass. I take a slow draw out of my cigarette and look over at Mike who seems to be tired. "Long day Mike?" He just nods and smiles. I glance over at yippee and her stud for the night, and, of course, he's trying to do a tonsillectomy with his tongue.

It's too bad that drunken Jim is one of the smartest people at this bar right now. My opinions are becoming more solidified about people. A room full of people trying to impress with words that don't mean anything. People constantly push their stories and beliefs on you when you try to just sit and have a drink without wanting to talk to anyone. I've been coming into Mike's Place for a couple of years now just to release the stress from my own job. I hear people rant and complain about stupid things all day long. How the company I work for cheats this old piece of crap woman out of quarter every month to the idiot that can't read a freakin' bill. I am the consummate customer service scourge.

My dealings with ignorant people on a continual basis are diminishing my IQ, but somehow this place has always been a haven for me. I feel the stress leave my body with every sip of the Blue Moon I take of every pint glass. I always limit myself to two pints of Blue Moon every time I come in here so I don't end up like some of the drunks that I have, over the years, come to despise. I do enough to release stress and move on, which at this moment will be soon. I see that yippee Sheila and her stud have left toward the back exit of the bar.

Her voice was starting to annoy me! Jim looks over and asks me if I would kick her out of bed. "No, if I could just duct tape her mouth shut." Jim chuckles, slams the rest of his Bud down his throat, throws some dead presidents on the bar and slowly walks out the back door behind Sheila and her boy toy. With Jim gone I have a moment to myself where I could look at the TV and see more of this clown Bowman.

It just seems recently that more politicians get their positions by how they look rather than any substance they have to offer. It's too bad that we don't have anymore Lincoln's, Washington's, or Jackson's running the big show. We get the over the top Howdy Doody that has to have the right makeup and the perfect smile for the camera, getting political positions that a regular Joe should be getting. Where has this country gone?

What happened to the hard working man that had blisters on his hands from toiling the ground all day, and made enough so his family could eat and have a roof over their heads; to the knotted tie yuppie that sits behind a desk in his leather chair making millions while others do the hard work and get paid millions less? Well, like everything else nowadays it's in the presentation of looks for the most part and not the substance.

We live in a world where there is no thinking- it's all perception, and if your perception is good enough to sway, you rule. It goes back to the old story: In the land of the blind, the one-eyed man will be king. We have politicians being swayed by special interest groups and not by the passion of what he believes.

This land was built on hard work, sweat, blood, and a firm belief of helping our fellow man. Now look at this dump of a country! We have huge murder rates, rape victims, assault that's through the roof, and many more crimes against each other. Instead of embracing life, we see how much we can get away with and, consequently, hope we don't get caught. We have children being stalked by sick perverts roaming the streets because our prisons can't hold all these sick bastards.

There are people that believe children should be protected by their parents, but by us as a whole when these kids are in public. What responsibility did Bowman take when little Johnny got sodomized and murdered by a man let out of prison three months earlier, the perp was one of "Governor Bowman's get out of jail free pardons," one of twenty five he gave convicted criminals. He calls it a misjudgment. I call it a travesty! I love this land of opportunity, but it's scum like Bowman that have made this country the sick place it is, then again people like Bowman are more common anymore. I would do anything to better the United States of America, and that's why when I cast my vote for President of the United States, it will not be for Senator Bowman!

I like to vote for someone, but in this case it will also be a vote against that sick bastard. I want a candidate that is passionate for what he believes in and can convince me of our commitment to make this a better country, not a politician without feeling or beliefs of his own. How can Bowman look at

Johnny's family and not want to vomit? I know I did when that camera zoomed in on him introducing himself at Johnny's funeral. How that scum has no heart is beyond me. Many stories follow this idiot Bowman, and I'm sure there are more stories that I haven't even heard yet.

I have half a pint of Blue Moon left and slowly take another sip. I knock a few more ashes into the ashtray, and think of my incredible problem. My friend Nate from work told me that it was the weirdest thing he's ever seen. Janet Stevens is a supervisor where I work, she is very rude and cruel at times. I don't know if she suffers from a huge dose of penis envy, but it is obvious that with her being a woman, she feels it necessary to keep up with the men in the industry by over compensating with the attitude and cruelty.

It is a false sense of security, but since she isn't my supervisor, I really don't care. Nate sits next to me at work and around 2 p.m. Janet comes strutting behind us to Mary's desk which is three work spaces down from me, and waits until she gets off the phone with a customer. What started as a gentle conversation soon becomes a battle of words. Mary has tears streaming down her face and looks as though she feels so helpless. Nothing Mary says can get her out of the talons of Janet.

Nate leans over my shoulder and tells me he thinks Mary should hit her. I lean back to Nate and say that she will, in about one minute lay Janet out cold with one punch. I look at this scene of verbal abuse from Janet. By then, I am so involved in this horrid match of words, I feel she is screaming at me. My limit has come to where I can't take anymore and I picture myself driving my fist through Janet's face. I free my mind of the situation and see Mary standing over Janet's laid out body on the floor. Janet's blood was dripping off Mary's knuckles and a sense of shock came over Mary's face like she had no control of what she had just done.

Nate smiles, and says:

"Joel, you are whacked dude! How did you know Mary was going to do that?"

"It was just a guess, Nate. I had this feeling that Janet would push it too far this time, and she did. I feel I can make people do what I want. I'm not sure if it is a prediction, or if I can make people do things by controlling their actions. When it happens, I feel it happens to me depending on the intensity of the situation."

"Joel, is this the first time you ever predicted something like this?"

Those words haunt me even now. I keep thinking about it, even though it happened hours ago. Have I had this happen before? I keep thinking over the past couple of years about stupid things that have happened where I thought maybe I predicted the outcome, but I couldn't. Then it hits me. I do remember some instances when I was growing up in Muncie.

There was a girl named Jill that I would say I had a little crush on in the third grade. She was a real cute girl for an 8 year old, but she couldn't stand me. I had the most horrendous case of cooties, just ask her. Months went by during the school year, and Jill still couldn't stand me. I remember at recess one day I saw her with a few friends across the pavement as I sat under a tree trying to sketch some sort of picture I can't recall.

Anyway, she looks over at me, and our eyes meet. I think of how great it would be if she would quit being mean to me, and if she would just kiss me in front of all these kids. I close my eyes thinking about it, intensely hoping it would happen. When my eyes open I see Jill right in front of me. Her eyes close and she plants a small kiss right on my lips. It was very innocent, but

Jill still reminds me to this day that she felt as though she had no control over herself when she did that.

She says that she felt like a puppet and did what the puppet master wanted. Jill says to this day that any man that can make her that weak in the knees deserves to have her. She is now my girlfriend and I keep dragging my feet on the whole marriage thing, but I don't think I could run the risk of losing her by having her move in with me. I am the biggest slob, I hate a lot of people, and I'm constantly angry with something.

I would say that Jill knows me better than anyone, (and has for 19 years), but what she doesn't realize is that I may be that puppet master she described. I have thoughts like these on occasion and wonder if I'm going out of my mind, if I may have a gift, or if I am cursed. I usually shrug these racing thoughts out of my head until I bury my face into a pint glass, and those thoughts race through my head once more. I look up at Mike as I finish my Blue Moon. I throw down a Hamilton and walk towards the back door to go home and meet Nate for the game tonight.

"Hey Joel, you want a coke?"

"Sure Nate."

While he was gone I check the voicemail I received. Aww, it's Jill. *I just wanted to call and tell you I love you. I hope your night with Nate is going well.* I wonder how her day went. I wish I were there with my baby Jill. She is the best thing that has ever happened to a poor sap like me. I hate basketball, but I did tell Nate I would go if one of his girls couldn't make it tonight. At least Nate gave me a couple days notice and not last minute. Our hometown team isn't doing well tonight. I see that the Bucks have opened up a twenty two point lead on us now and it's getting close to the fourth quarter. Nate comes back all smiles and hands me a coke.

"Joel, want to have some fun tonight?"

"What kind of fun… I don't think I like that sinister smile you have right now Nate."

"You know that thing you do Joel… Why not try it here and have some fun?"

I just shake my head and smile. There was no way I was going to do that. It was too much effort. Every time I predict something, it's like I end up being one of those crystal ball gypsies that end up being shunned for their twenty dollar predictions. On the other hand, since I hate basketball, this could be entertaining for me. Nate is so into the Pacers, it is kind of disgusting. He looks toward the floor with an intense type of look as though he wants to be playing instead of watching.

The point guard for the Bucks trips and loses the ball. Miller picks it up and drives in for an easy lay-up. Milwaukee brings it up and a pass that should go to someone from that Bucks team is errant and goes out of bounds. Everyone in the arena is wondering where he was going with that pass. I know where it was going and start to smile. Nate looks over and smacks the back of my head and says if I start doing things like that I need to tell him. I say, "Watch this…" the point guard for the Bucks gets the ball and stops. He just hands the ball to Miller and he takes the ball and slams it. Nate laughs so hard he has tears coming down his face.

I am finally realizing that I don't foresee the future. I am the future. I can make any one person do what I want, when I want. It seems that I can control voluntary functions, but to what extent, I don't know. I hate using this power because every time I use it, I lose something. It feels as though I lose a part of my life and slowly die a little. Every time I use it, my body feels as though I ran a marathon, but the weird thing is, once I get a couple hours of rest, I'm fine. When Mary jacked Janet the other day I was exhausted. For a good two hours I was completely out of it. It is very hard to describe.

Nate smacks the back of my head and asks me why I've stopped the Barnum and Bailey basketball game. I look up and do my thing. A bad pass here, and a dribble off the foot, a shot from thirty feet out. I keep doing these hilarious things on the court that no one can tell what I am doing, and Nate is laughing and crying so hard I think he's going to wet himself.

He glances over at me, his eyes get really wide, like a deer in headlights and tells me that I am so pale I look dead. I tell Nate I'm extremely tired and need to go. He nods his head with his eyes wide open, covers me with his jacket and helps me out. We leave the arena and get outside. It's there that I tell Nate what I can do and what the side effects are. I tell Nate I need to sit and rest and then plop myself down on a bench right outside the arena. I proceed to tell him everything and, instead of having sympathy for me, he gets a huge smile and says, "You know what this means?"

"What does this mean Nate?"

"That we will be millionaires!"

"How can that be?"

"You can control a game Joel. You know what kind of money we could make betting on games you throw?"

"Didn't think of it that way Nate."

"Joel, I have a bookie so that won't be a problem. I'll take care of the finances part. You just worry about making sure Manning throws eight touchdown passes a game this upcoming fall."

I smile, then tell Nate, "If I had known this twenty years ago Nate, the Colts would be on their twentieth consecutive Super Bowl win."

Nate laughs with tears in his eyes and agrees. He can't stop laughing! Is he laughing because he had just found his golden goose? Do I trust Nate with this kind of information? I tell Nate that he can't tell a soul about this and he agrees. My mind wonders and I start thinking about Jill and that terrible job she's in. I haven't seen her happy in a long time and maybe making some quick money might get her out of that office of hers and make her somewhat happy. Her boss, David is such an abusive person. I wish I could destroy that man, but my Jill tells me she can handle it, so I back off.

I look at Nate and he glances up toward me and tells me I'm getting the color back in my face. I keep thinking that Nate and I will be rich. I don't think of myself as greedy, but I do like the idea of making enough for Jill to be comfortable and not so stressed all the time. I think about this power I have and wonder what God was thinking by giving me this dubious power.

My thoughts race as I get up and walk towards the car with Nate walking slowly next to me. Nate keeps asking me if I'm alright and I keep telling him I'll use my power on him if he doesn't shut up. I look at him and he's white as a sheet now and then I chuckle and tell him I was just kidding. He wasn't worth knocking any time off my life. Nate is a good person and has a good heart, but he has a tendency to be greedy…and he is so easy to pick on.

I ask Nate if he wants to go to the pub across the way and finish the game. Nate asks why I'm interested in going. I tell him that I need to see if my "power" can change somebody's action through a TV. He grabs my arm and we start jogging to the pub. Nate doesn't let go of this vice grip on my arm until we reach the door. Manny's is a quaint little pub that doesn't have too many people in it this time of night. Since the game was still going on I guess I can believe Manny's not being too busy. Nate and I sit down to watch the fourth quarter and Nate orders us both a Bud. Immediately Nate starts digging at me.

"Okay Joel, it's time to get to work!"

I sit there trying to get Redd to throw an errant pass. It doesn't work. I think I might not be concentrating hard enough. I end up trying again with no positive result. I look at Nate and he stares at me with anticipation.

"Nate, it's not working no matter how hard I try. It looks like we'll need to get season tickets."

"Joel, where am I going to get money for that?"

"Nate, listen, if I can take my savings and put all of it on the next game I'm sure you can do the same. We just need to get tickets."

"Tickets won't be a problem Joel. It's my savings. I don't have much, only about five hundred dollars. You have to promise me you can change the outcome. If you do, I'll be indebted to you for life."

"Don't worry about that. I just need you to keep your mouth shut about this."

"No problem Joel. I would lose just as much as you if this were to get out."

Nate had a point. What would we both have to gain if this did leak out? I could always tell everyone that I didn't have this power and nobody would think twice, but it could keep me out of seeing live sporting events. For once, Nate made sense. My circus act before the fourth quarter brought the Pacers back and now we have a good game with no intervention from me.

I missed Jill all day. It was about 10 p.m. and I drive into Jill's apartment complex and see her car there. I pull in and park next to her. My pride and joy is a new Monte Carlo that is pewter looking in color and so much fun to drive. I get out of the car and walk toward Jill's door. As I fumble through my keys to get to hers I hear something behind her door as if she's talking on the phone. I simply knock not wanting to startle her by opening the door myself. She opens the door and a soft smile invites me in as well as a big hug and kiss. Jill proceeds to tell me she got off the phone with her mom and told her some news today which happened at work. She asks me if I was planning to spend the night. I nod and ask her what had happened at work today. Jill's big green eyes start to well up with tears and she apologizes to me for not telling me sooner.

"Tell me what sooner, Jill?"

"David crossed the line with me today Baby. I'm filing sexual harassment charges on him."

"What? How long has this been going on?"

"It has been for years Joel. Please, don't be mad at me."

"What kind of proof do you have?"

She leads up to her proof by telling me what happened at the office today. David Johns has been Jill's boss for the last eight years. He brought her in after she completed one year at Ball State. David is very arrogant and his presence in a room is very intimidating. He is one of the best lawyers in Indianapolis. His peers say he is cutthroat, but always goes by the book. David has a reputation of getting what he wants and if he doesn't get it, watch out.

Jill tells me that David yelled at her when files that should have been on his desk were not there. She said it was an honest mistake, but David just snapped at her. Jill told me the lines David said to her:

"Jill, I have brought you into this company and molded you into what you are today. Your work is outstanding, but lately it has been very poor. If you don't start doing things the right way, Jill, your job could be given to another poor nineteen year old desperate to prove themselves. Keep in mind that everyone is expendable!"

Tongue lashings towards her were not rare in his office and she has been used to them over the years. David has used his power to create a constant fear in her. Jill's first couple years with him were a hell on earth ordeal for her because he knows just how to get to Jill. He has tried to make sexual advances to her many times, but she never gave in to any of them. Jill says she left his office struggling not to cry. She rushed to the bathroom which is about fifteen feet from David's office and composed herself for her day of hell. She says that she looked into the mirror and stared intently into her eyes for what seemed like an hour, but in reality was probably no more than five minutes. A stare is one thing, but this stare was a stare of strength. She always coward to his loud disposition, and feared him deeply. Lawyers tremble like she does just at his very presence, but not this time.

She continues her story saying her intense stare pierces deeply into the mirror as if it could cut the glass. Jill finally decides that it is time to release her revenge on David. Revenge has been the oldest motivation in the history of human existence and has brought out evil in most that have worn the crown. Jill says how intense she was while leaving the bathroom and stops by Ashley's desk. Ashley is one of Jill's dearest and trusted friends.

Ashley has been a clerk for David's firm for almost six years. Jill trained her when she came in and they have been close ever since. If they didn't have each other they would have left the firm years ago. Jill tells me that she went to Ashley's desk and went off about David yelling at her again. Ashley asked what happened and she said that he just went too far this time with threatening her job over something that she didn't deserve to be yelled at for. She told Ashley to meet her at the Starbucks across the street from the office for lunch. Jill told her that she was going to see a lawyer friend about her potential case.

Once Jill arrived at Starbucks they both walked out the side exit and went to the park for a few minutes and when Jill found out Ashley had taken the rest of the day off, they went for some Chinese food, picked up a bottle of wine and came back to the apartment. I end up asking Jill how long David has been making sexual advances to her:

"When did this all start Jill?"

"About five years ago?"

"Why didn't you tell me about any of this Jill?"

"Didn't think I'd have the guts to follow through, so I hid it thinking it would go away, but it never has. Every time that I thought it was gone, David would make a horrendous pass at me that brought back the feelings of fear, anger and hatred again. I always feared that I would lose my job by rejecting him, and I always wondered why I never did."

"Because of what you are going to do now, that's why! If he fired you he knew you would go for his throat on a sexual harassment charge and with David being married and having four kids, it wouldn't make it easy on him with his wife."

"I always wanted to tell Joanna (David's wife), but I always feared she would tell David which would put me in a deeper hole."

Jill was on the brink of burying the most popular lawyer in Indianapolis and I understand that it will be terrifying for her. She is going up against David Johns? David and Goliath is a squirt gun fight compared to this and it seemed to finally register with me. I asked her if she would be ready to go to trial. Jill told me she was looking to settle, and didn't know if she could handle a trial. I told her that David was so arrogant that he would get on the stand just because of his powerful demeanor. She started to cry and a sudden burst of fear overwhelmed her as she sat motionless thinking of her future.

I mentioned to her that we could always move away from Indianapolis if it gets ugly and that spending time away from Indy wouldn't be such a bad thing. I wipe the tears away from her cheeks as I tell her that it's not fair for her to be treated this way. Jill has always been a good person. Jill tears up again when she realizes what this could do to her mom and dad.

Her dad has a slight heart condition which I know could be

intensified with stress from this possible trial. Her mom is a quiet woman who doesn't like to be bothered with the outside world too much. Jill's mom is quite a homebody and has been her whole life. While her dad worked, her mom stayed home with Jill and her two sisters (Jill being the oldest). She doesn't know how bad it can be on the outside. She sees television and movies, but it's not the same as when you experience the world from outside your own living room. Jill has tried unsuccessfully to get her mom to work part time, so she could get out of the house and feel as though she is worth something.

All of the girls are gone from home now and two are married, so it makes sense for her mom to get out and start a life of her own. Jill is the last girl to be single, but her parents love me. They know deep down I will ask Jill someday for her hand in marriage, but they don't want to push it.

I look across the floor and see tapes and an empty wine bottle. I've known Jill and Ashley's ritual for years now and know they are very close, but I tell Jill:

"Are you sure you want Ash to know all this stuff since she does work in the same office?"

"She is encouraging me to go for it. Ash has been so supportive, Joel. She actually told me to tell you as soon as I could because you had to know everything that is going on. I tried to sleep a couple of hours ago, but my heart ached not knowing how you would take this."

"Maybe I should hear some of these tapes before I form an opinion."

I started one of the tapes and heard the following:

"Jill you know I have brought you in the company with every intention of moving you up. The question is Jill, how fast do you want to move up the ladder?"

"David, stop touching me! I enjoy working here, but I don't want this!"

"*Jill, you are a very attractive girl and you should have the best things in life. I'm offering you advancement here as well as a huge pay increase.*"

"*What, if I sleep with you?*"

"*I didn't say it like that, Jill*"

"*You didn't have to, David! For the last time get your hands off me. Your advances are unwarranted and I will never sleep with you! If it means my job, then fine! You need to sleep this off. You are drunk and your breath is horrendous from all that alcohol.*"

"*C'mon Jill.*"

"*David, no! What would your wife think of this!?*"

All of the sudden there is silence and you hear someone walking, and a door closing. There is more silence and then the recording stops.

"Are all the tapes like this, Jill?"

"Pretty much."

"Are these all the recordings?"

"They're copies. I gave the originals to my lawyer handling this. I also handed over some video tapes from a few company parties we had in the office. "

"You have this bastard on videotape, too?"

"Yes, and I will never show you those, Joel. You would *kill* him if I showed you those."

Jill looks at me knowing that I'm trying to muster some sort of opinion. I was still thinking about my night with Nate, and now this.

"Jill, I have always supported your decisions in everything. You are a bright woman and I know I'm very lucky to have you. Your sense of reason is better than mine. I must say if this is what you have started to pursue… then pursue it."

"But how do you feel about it? What's your opinion?"

"I hope that his wife will get everything. Destroy him!"

Jill leans over with a tear in her eye and flashes a huge smile. A smile that I had not seen since she moved back from Ball State. She moved back in with her parents after hating campus life and not showing any motivation for decent grades. She blames a lot of things for her failure at college life, but deep down I know she hated being away from me. She said she missed me the entire time she was there. She couldn't eat, sleep or even concentrate in class because she was so madly in love with me.

For the last eight years David has been tough on Jill and it has taken a toll on her both physically and mentally. An outsider can look at the way he treats her and know that he uses her. He knows she would have a difficult time trying to find a job since this is the only job she has had. It really upsets me that she is going through all this.

Jill still occasionally attends the church she grew up in and used to teach Sunday school to youngsters. It's where her parents are still active. Jill was raised in the Baptist church and has always been a very good girl. I started attending her church when my parents died. She never drank, smoked, cussed or did any drugs while growing up and still doesn't except for the occasional bottle of wine she drinks with Ashley.

She kisses me softly on my lips and then gives me a huge hug. I then tell her that if she needs me for anything during this, just let me know.

Jill is the most wonderful woman I have ever known. It goes back to what I've always said about people that do bad things, using other people to get power. They think they can get away with the wrongdoing. Why is it that the innocent are always the ones played like pawns in a chess match? They do not wrong anyone, yet they are the ones to foster a bad person's greed, lust, revenge and fame.

David Johns must be destroyed before he preys on another helpless soul for his own personal gain. I think back in history to the Roman Empire and how it was destroyed, not by an outside force, but from within. How the seven deadly sins hovered over Rome like the grim reaper waits to consume a dying man, and then all seven were released on Rome like a gun going off to start an Olympic track meet.

Isn't it funny how centuries go by and a majority of people know how and why certain things happen in history to civilizations, countries and the destruction of mad men. How can we go through all these years not learning from historical facts? Take the United States as a perfect example. Our destruction will not be at the hand of another country, it will most certainly come from within.

Who goes to sleep without locking their doors? Who goes out at night and walks the streets of any downtown city and feels safe? Who keeps themselves at arms length from their neighbor because we don't know their history? Jill is the prey of a power hungry animal that will destroy her if given the chance. David has done evil and must pay for it. I know Jill will be harassed by everyone, including the media, but this is right and she knows it must be done, as do I.

"Jill, how did your mom take the news?"

"Okay, but she cried."

"I understand how tough it could be on her. Does your dad know, or are you going to pick a time to tell him together? With his heart condition and all; I don't know if telling him right now would be good for him."

"I know Joel. I've thought about telling my dad, but I need him through all this. I need you just as much, Joel, if not more."

"I'm always here Jill. You know that. I just don't want anymore secrets like this being kept from me."

Jill brushes back her shoulder length blonde hair and says, "I know, Baby, and I am so sorry if I hurt you. It was one of those things that I tried not to think about. I thought it would go away. Well, it never did."

I kiss Jill and we go to bed. Jill turns on the portable TV to ESPN and the headline story is about the "Pacer-Bucks Circus". Berman goes into detail about the occurrences in the third quarter.

"Joel, why didn't you tell me about this?"

"I didn't have a chance to! You had to tell me about that walking gland you work for, so it kind of slipped my mind."

Jill chuckles and we look at the craziness in the replays. She can't believe what she's seeing and her mouth drops during the highlights. Jill has always been a sports fan. The Colts, Pacers, Redwings and Reds are her favorites from the big four; she has more knowledge about sports history and trivia than I do. My Jill is the best catch for any man out there. What guy doesn't want a girl that is desirous of being married at the fifty yard line during the halftime of a Colts game? That's Jill, she's beautiful, smart and loves sports. A guys dream comes true and I'm living the dream.

"So, how was your day Joel?"

"Not bad."

"Jill, I have something to tell you."

"What is it? Are you okay?"

"I'm fine... it's just...."

"It's just what, Joel?"

"You know the highlights you saw of the Pacer game? I caused all the craziness."

"You mean the crazy shots, bad passes and dribbles out of bounds?"

"Uh- yeah."

She laughs at me!

"Joel, you're living in fantasy land."

"I bet I can make you do something you don't want to do."

"Like what?"

I look at her and she gets on her knees in bed, holds her hand out and slaps me right across the face. She looks at me in horror.

"Joel I'm so sorry. I don't know what came over me."

"I did that, Jill. I wanted you to slap me. I know you would never think of striking me and I did that to prove to you what I did on the court tonight. I'm sorry, but I had to do that or you would never believe me. I can't believe it myself. I told you no more secrets. I didn't want to wait while you go through this ordeal at work and then keep finding excuses for not telling you about this ability."

Jill looks at me as if I told her I found the key to eternal peace on earth. Her mind is racing and every thought that channels through her mind, shoots out through her mouth. She talks of life, death, hunger, emotions and feelings are mentioned. She describes many different scenarios with different twists and then she stops.

"Have you used this power to kill, or hurt anyone?"

"No, just pretty much the game tonight and at work the other day."

"What happened at work?"

"You know Mary?"

"Yes I do, I think. Does she have long, dark hair, and tiny in stature?"

"Yeah, she belted Janice dead center in the face. Mary was fired for it and Janice is still in the hospital, I think with some sort of nasal problem from the hit."

"Are you upset you had a part in it?"

"Kind of, but Janet deserved it. Mary losing her job wasn't right. Janet was in her face screaming and, from what I know, still has her position when she gets better."

"Does anyone else know of this power you have?"

"Just Nate."

"Nate! That selfish idiot! How could you tell him!? If there's anyone to bring you down, it's him."

"Whatever, I trust him and that's all there is to it. C'mon, who's going to believe him if he tells them I have some sort of special power to make people do things they don't want to. Sweetheart, with everything you're going through now, this should be the least of your worries."

"What is that supposed to mean?"

"I don't want you worrying about me, that's all. I can handle it."

Jill looks at me and calmly smiles. She tells me she needs to get some sleep so she can be in the office on time tomorrow. I kiss her gently on the lips and I turn off the light.

I can hear Jill in the bedroom struggling to get out of bed. She must have smelled that heavenly coffee I made. I take a sip from my cup as she walks in. Her hair is messed up and her beautiful green eyes are barely showing through the two slits from her eyelids. Jill doesn't say a word as she pours herself some coffee and comes to the kitchen table to sit down. I keep reading the paper and hope she notices what's on the table.

"Joel! You didn't forget! You remembered how much I love these!"

She screamed so loud I almost fell over from the shock. I got up this morning and got her the cinnamon rolls from Coles Bakery that she absolutely adores. I bought her favorite bag of Kona coffee and picked up a newspaper. With everything she went through yesterday, I figured I would be the great boyfriend and get her ready for a day that I know she is dreading. She gets up for more coffee this time as she looks at the bag, she asks me why I went all out. She chuckles, "What do you want Joel?"

"Why, can't I just be a good boyfriend?"

"I'm not saying you shouldn't be. What's the occasion?"

"I just know you are having a rough time and I wanted to at least make your morning enjoyable."

Jill comes to the table and sits in my lap, and plants a kiss on my mouth. While she sits there I ask her, "When is the best time of the year to get married?"

She looks at me as if I were kidding.

"You know I have always wanted to marry you Jill. What cut of diamond do you like Baby?"

"You are serious!?"

"Yes I am. Why wouldn't I want to marry you? You are everything I have ever wanted and needed in a woman and to top it off, you are my best friend."

She gives me another huge smile and plants another kiss on my mouth. I look at her and she reaches across the table, rips a cinnamon roll off the block of six that I bought her and shoves it in her mouth which is comical because this roll is almost as big as her head. Jill takes a huge bite and throws the rest on the table, trying to talk with a mouth full of roll and white icing.

"What are you trying to say, Jill?"

She takes a sip of coffee to get some of the roll down.

"I want a princess cut, Joel!"

"Well, my budget will only allow so much."

"What does that mean?"

"I'm not a rich man. You know that!"

"So a five carat diamond is out of the question?"

"I'm afraid so…"

"Whatever you choose, Joel, I will love it because you picked it."

"How many cracker jack boxes do you think I need to buy 'til I find the ring you want? I have about a hundred bucks."

Jill looks at me, smirks and without warning takes that quarter eaten roll and shoves the icing in my face.

"I'm sorry honey, but it sounded as though you were going to get my engagement ring out of a crackerjack box."

"I wasn't until you did that! You better watch it or I'll use my powers on you."

"That's not fair! You can't do that to me!"

After a few minutes of laughs and goofing around, Jill looks at the clock and squeals when she sees the time. She runs to the bathroom and starts the shower. I slowly calm back down, sit, and wipe the rest of the icing off my face while I read the headlines in the paper. It's Senator Bowman again in a typically huge, cheesy, color picture plastered all over the front page. The story talks about how he is leading the pack for the Democrats, and that his opposition has slowly admitted defeat. I can't believe this guy is the only one the Democrats could find worthy of the highest elected position in the world. I'm so disgusted that I take the Sports section out and read about the game I had a hand in the previous night.

I read the story and can't believe it was me that did all of those things. I shake my head in disbelief that the few things I did made the lead story in the Sports section. I hear Jill singing in the shower and laugh; it's such a shame that she can't hit a note to save her life. After chuckling a bit at Jill's karaoke imitation, I read the rest of the Sports section and see that the Pacers are three wins from winning their division.

Jill comes out of the shower obviously in a hurry. She gets dressed quickly, dries her hair and tries to talk to me at the same time. I tell her I have the day off and plan to make a trip to the library to research a bit about the condition I have. She seems to be supportive of it and appears to be taking it better than I ever imagined. Jill has a lot on her mind now, so I'm sure my quandary is taking somewhat of a backseat to her problems.

It doesn't bother me, but at the same time she acts as though she already knew I had this power. That somehow she knew before I did. Just a weird feeling I can't put my finger on. Jill comes out fully dressed in a black skirt and silky white top. She hops across the floor putting her shoes on.

"Have a good day, Baby. Don't get lost at the library."

"Funny, Jill…. Make sure Mr. Octopus keeps his tentacles off you."

"What did you say?!"

"His tentacles Jill… not testicles"

Jill comes over, smiles and kisses me goodbye and I see her out the door. After boxing up her rolls and cleaning the coffee maker, I leave for the library.

Who goes to the library on such a wonderful, sunny, spring day? That would be me. I get out of my car, put some money in the meter and head toward the downtown library. My first thought is that I might be able to find a book which lists some people with the same ability I possess, but then I think about how possible it is that someone may have never had this power documented and I will end up not finding what I need.

I keep wondering if the closest people around me wonder if I am going crazy, or if I am obsessed with finding out how much this power can do, or take out of me. As I walk through the front door I head toward a computer to begin my research. After about twenty minutes, I find four books that look like winners. *Psychic and Paranormal Abilities* by Judith Barksdale is the first one that intrigues me. I go get the book and set up shop at a desk away from most people, so I can concentrate. My attention is drawn to the back cover:

Judith Barksdale graduated from Harvard with a Bachelor's Degree in Psychology in 1963, and obtained a

Masters Degree in Psychology from Brown in 1968. Her PhD came in 1972 from the University of Virginia. Psychotic Behavior and the Paranormal was Judith's first publication, she has written two other books. Unimaginable and Psychic and Paranormal

Abilities are both thought provoking and a relentless pursuit of the psychologically unknown. She is now retired and living in Asheville, North Carolina.

I flip through the index and search for something intriguing. My eyes focus on a chapter called *Control*. Maybe this is the chapter I need to be looking at. I start reading and then the words in the chapter jump up and catch me:

Through my research and studies I have come to believe that there are people in this world that have an ability to control a person's mind and thoughts.

After reading further and skimming a few more chapters, I realize that I want to visit Judith, but can't find the time with my work and Jill's problems. I have to find out if she has done any research on those who have the ability to control another's body with thought. I read further and examine a passage that is very interesting.

The voluntary and involuntary functions of one's body have always caught my interest. How can a man stand, walk, and maintain a constant motion, but have no control over his beating heart?

My mind wonders if I have the ability to control ones ability to live. Do I have the power to kill just by hoping I can stop a beating heart? I end up at the counter to check out the Judith Barksdale book and make my way out the door. My car is still soaking up the sun. As I put the book in the trunk, I look up the street to the little jewelry shop on the corner. Closing the trunk I walk to the coffee shop next to the jeweler and get a cup of coffee before heading over to look at Jill's "Cracker Jack" ring.

My eyes open wide when I see the prices on the princess cut diamonds. I figured I could get a nice diamond for around a grand. I keep looking and see a three carat in a platinum setting for around six and a half grand. I hate jewelry, but this ring did catch my eye. The jeweler asks for her ring size, and I tell him. He comes up to me and asks me my name and I tell him.

"Are you interested in putting this one on layaway?"

"Why not? I need to get this one anyway. It's a very classy looking ring."

"Very good selection Mr. Warner."

"I hope she likes it."

"She will."

I can't believe that I need to put down six hundred fifty bucks just to put it on layaway! Nate and I are definitely going to a few Pacer games very soon! I hope Nate put our bet in for the game Sunday. Maybe I should call him later and check on it.

Mr. Jeweler gives me a receipt and tells me I have to put a payment on the ring every month, or he will have the right to sell it to someone else. I don't think Mr. Jeweler knows that this ring will be paid for in cash by the middle of next week. As I leave the jeweler I feel like walking to Jill's office to see how she's doing today. It's only a block or so away.

My eyes slowly move toward the top of a monstrosity of a building and I realize that I am at Jill's office. I walk up to the guard at the front desk and tell him who I am and he calls up to see if they know me where Jill works. After a two minute wait Jill comes down with a smile on her face and gives me a hug. She tells me that it's been a good day. David has been out of the office all day and that nobody expects him in the rest of the afternoon. Jill asks me if I found anything out at the library and I tell her I had an enlightening experience.

"What did you find out?"

"I have been thinking about how to use my power for good and not evil."

"Okay, now what gave you this enlightenment?"

"A woman called Judith Barksdale wrote a book which opened my eyes a bit, but it really didn't delve into any particular situation that was associated with my problem."

"Well, Baby, I have to get back to work. Meet me at my apartment….. Please?!"

"Okay, I'll be there when you get home from work."

Jill turns and almost skips with glee to the elevator. She turns and smiles at me as she enters the box on a rope. I hate those things! I never did like elevators when I was young and hate them even more so now. As I head out the door I see Ashley walk in and we chat for a moment. I tell her to visit Jill's apartment around 7p.m.

"I'm cooking dinner for you and Jill tonight."

"No way! Since when do you know how to cook Joel?"

"Hey now! I have always made a mean mac and cheese, Ash!"

"I'll be there. See ya later."

I walk the block and a half back to my car and pick up some groceries on the way.

The finishing touches are almost done. A nice breast of chicken in a honey glaze that I created, asparagus tips with garlic butter sauce and a caesar salad to start things off. I hear a car pull into the parking lot outside. It sounds like Jill's car and I hope she didn't stop at McDonalds on the way home.

I wait for her by the door as I hear the keys rustling in the deadbolt. Jill walks in with half a burger hanging out of her mouth and a McDonald's bag in hand as she takes the keys out of the deadbolt with the other. Her eyes close as she takes a huge whiff of what is cooking.

"How could you go to McDonalds!?"

She frees her hand from the keys and takes the burger out of her mouth.

"I didn't know you were cooking!"

"Zo, I just wanted it to be a surprise!"

"You surprised me alright! It smells heavenly. Joel, I know my last name is Zoeller, but I hate it when you call me Zo! I've told you that a million times!"

"I know you hate it, but I did it to get under your skin. Jill, I always do that when I'm upset with you."

About to take another bite of the burger, she spits what she had in her mouth into the bag, and, along with the rest of her uneaten meal, tosses it in the trash.

"I'd rather have what you're cooking. What is it that you are whipping together?"

In my best snooty maitre de voice, I say, "We are having a lovely honey glazed chicken breast, asparagus tips with garlic butter sauce and caesar salad to start."

"Sounds yummy, Babe."

Jill walks back to her room, taking her clothes off and slips into sweats and a baby tee. She comes back out and takes another huge whiff of the food.

"After seeing that burger in your mouth I'm guessing Ashley didn't tell you I invited her."

"No, I didn't see her till the last five minutes of the day, and even then she seemed in a hurry."

"I hope she doesn't forget, Jill. You know how she can be sometimes."

Jill sits on the kitchen counter as I stir the garlic sauce. She gets up and looks in the refrigerator and sees the bottle of wine I bought for this rare occasion.

"Chardonnay is a very excellent selection Joel. Do you need any help, Hon?

"I'm fine, just waiting for Ash."

As soon as I say that, a knock on the door startles us. Jill answers the door and invites Ashley in.

"Oh my, Joel, that doesn't smell like mac and cheese."

"It's a stunning array of Indianapolis' finest poultry and vegetables, Ash."

I ask the girls if they would set the table and they start pulling dishes out of the cupboards and silverware out of the drawers.

My incredible dinner is about to disappear into the stomachs of three hungry people. After the girls finish setting the table they sit and start chatting about work.

I start by bringing out the caesar salad. As soon as it hits the table Ashley declares she is starving and dives into the salad as though she hasn't seen food in days. As the salad gets passed around the table, I ask Ashley how her day went and she just gives me a 'so-so' sign with her hand. She proceeds to tell us that she spent all day at the courthouse and at the library. I told her that I was there before I ran into her.

"How weird is that? I just left the library and walked from there since it wasn't too far from the office. I can't believe I didn't run into you."

"Me either, I was there for about an hour doing some research."

"Anything interesting?"

"Just checking on a few things that intrigue me."

Jill is so into her salad that she doesn't seem to be paying attention to anything Ash and I are talking about. We all start our salads as I keep looking at the stove from where I'm sitting just to make sure nothing burns. As I finish up my salad, I walk out to the kitchen and get the main course ready. After pouring the garlic butter sauce on the asparagus I bring the main course out to the dining table.

The girls look in shock as though they never expected me to cook such a wonderful dinner. After Jill and Ashley serve themselves the chicken and asparagus, I open the bottle of Chardonnay that I had chilled in the fridge and pour each of us a glass. We all start eating and not a word is said while dining on, what I have to say, is the best meal I've ever made.

"That was a slice of heaven, Joel."

"I second it!"

"Thanks girls, I really appreciate it. It was good, wasn't it? I don't think it's as good as my mac and cheese, but it will do."

Jill throws her napkin at me and smiles as she starts cleaning off the table. Ashley is close behind helping her with the leftovers. I get up and plop down on the sofa to turn on the TV for a moment. All I see are videos of Senator Bowman shaking hands and kissing babies.

I start flipping through channels until I get to ESPN and then Jill comes from the kitchen and fixates on the headline news they have. It ends up being a piece on the Yankees and how they haven't produced so far this year. Jill slowly walks back into the kitchen and picks up her conversation with Ashley. After about five minutes I hear Ashley's keys jingle.

"Great meal, Joel. I have to get going. I'm meeting some guy at Mike's Place tonight."

"Be careful, Ashley."

I wave to her as she leaves. Jill finishes at the kitchen sink as Ashley shuts the door behind her and comes out to join me on the sofa. Jill asks me if the Reds won today and I answer with a yes.

"Help me to understand this, Jill. We've known each other all this time and I've never asked you why you like the Reds. What is it about them?"

"Well, they're close to Indy and my dad used to take me to games at Riverfront when I was a little girl. He is from Cincinnati you know."

"Why would you cheer for a team that blows?"

"Hey, mister, when they win the World Series this year, you won't say that!"

I chuckle and giggle at Jill's non-threatening defense of a crappy team. Deep down I've always liked the Reds, but never told Jill. It has kept our springs and summers entertaining. The

Reds would be a great team if they could just get some decent pitching. It's like I always tell Jill, "Pitching wins pennants."

"What is it about the Reds you don't like?"

"I do like them, but their GM sucks. He doesn't get what they need."

"What do they need, Hon?"

"Pitching, pitching and more pitching. They have the hitting, but you won't win a World Series with 15-13 games. "

"Maybe you're right Joel. Let's go to bed and have some fun."

"Twist my arm, Baby."

Jill takes my hand and leads me to the bedroom and I close the door as if someone were going to walk in on us.

    I hope she reads my note. Jill hates it when I leave without saying goodbye, but I know she needs her rest after last night. Café Indy is my Saturday morning hangout. I get my newspaper and my Jamaica Blue Mountain coffee and read. This time I bring the Judith Barksdale book to read more about her findings. While flipping through the pages and drinking my coffee I find nothing about the condition I have. This book is written by a psychologist and the pages I read are fascinating, but not what I am looking for.

    She does have some comments that make me think that my ability has crossed her mind. Judith states that, there have been cases where some people have been given the gift of reading ones minds. Her insight is quite intriguing and she goes on to say that if this ability has been documented, then it stands to reason that there may be those that have had the skill to control someone's physical functions. It is a hypothesis I wasn't expecting to read, but it was very chilling to think this woman may have the information I need. I must visit her!

As I look up toward the counter I see a man order coffee. He turns and I realize it's Nate. I call out to him and, after paying; he grabs his coffee and joins me.

"What's up, Joel?"

"Not much, just reading a book, eager to find some information on the gift or curse that I have. By the way, I meant to call you last night and see if you placed our bet."

"It is done, my friend. We'll be rich by the end of spring."

Nate had a sheepish grin on his face while saying it. I ended up taking out some more of my savings and let Nate take care of our first bet. He asks me where I got fifty grand from and I told him it was part of my inheritance when my parents passed away. I told him that when we won I would give him a cut so he could make some jack the next time we bet. Nate smiled and said that he had to use outside sources because no bookie he knows would take a bet like that. He has friends with connections in Vegas and they placed the bet for him. I start getting nervous knowing my money is in the hands of strangers. Nate knows the look and says, "Trust me Joel. I know what I am doing."

"I hope. I just put a ring on layaway for Jill. I'm going to ask her to marry me next weekend."

"Congrats, buddy, where were you going to propose? If you don't have a place picked out, you could use the family's cabin up in Grand Rapids."

"I'll keep that in mind, Nate. I just want to get through tomorrow night and then I'll be able to think better."

"I hear ya, brother. Well, I'm out."

"See ya, Nate. I'll pick you up at six tomorrow night."

"Cool, later, Joel."

Nate is the cool one, but I do wonder if his intentions are good. We've known each other for years now and I don't think

I have ever seen Nate lose his composure. He has this boyish charm about him that makes him look simple, but at the same time he's dangerous because he is so smart. I just hope these people he's dealing with are legitimate. I feel a twinge of doubt, but I'm not hurting anyone by betting on a few games.

I keep flipping through pages trying to find another passage that jumps out at me, but I don't find it. With disgust I set aside the book and pick up the newspaper. The first thing I see, right on the front page, is Bowman's face. I don't want to get irritated yet, so I pull out the sports section and go through it quickly.

Jill will like the reality that the Reds finally made a trade to get some pitching. Jackson? No way. He's one of the best out there. I can't believe the Reds finally made a move toward greatness. It's not even a month into the season and the Reds have made one heck of a move.

My coffee is gone and I've had enough. I fold the newspaper and place it on top of the book and scurry out of the shop. Jill should be up by now.

I get back to Jill's, and as I pull into the parking lot, I see Ashley headed across the lot towards the stairs that lead to her apartment. Once I park the car, I get out and shout her name. She stops, turns and walks slowly toward me. I can tell she had a rough night and she looks as though someone has hit her. It also looks as though she has been crying. We talk for a moment and I guess this guy she met last night really liked her, and she ended up at his place. She is crying because he ended up kicking her out of his house, after a screaming match with him.

After chatting with Ashley a little, she heads up the stairs and I open Jill's door and find out Jill hasn't risen yet. I try to be quiet and get into bed with her. When I lift the sheets to get in she mumbles, "Where are you going?"

"No where, Jill, I just got here."

"What? You left already?"

"I did my Saturday ritual."

She still has her head on the pillow and mumbles some more, and as I lay down next to her she opens her eyes, our eyes meet and we talk for a little bit about some superficial things. Then I drop the bomb.

"Did you hear the Reds picked up Jackson in a trade?"

"Don't mess with me, Joel, I'm tired and I just woke up."

"I'm not kidding. It was in the paper. Must have happened after we went to bed last night."

I show her the story in the paper. Fully awake now, she struggles to get out of bed and sits up, paper in hand. She comments about how this Bowman guy looks cute. Where is she coming from? She told me she couldn't stand this guy. Jill looks at me after saying that and says, "Gotcha."

It was a sick joke, but Jill has always been like that. She was funny when she did it. Jill did get me that time. My parents were killed in a car accident, but by a drunk driver. The man driving the other car was a politician with no prior record of any substance abuse issues. That man was our wonderful Robert Bowman who was elected Governor of Indiana a year before the accident.

There was, of course, some press at the time, but throughout this election no one from any newspaper or television station has come to me wanting to know anything about how he destroyed my family, or how I handled being without parents right out of high school. I realize there is a slant in politics. That politicians and the media are pretty much in bed together. Bowman is a living example of how a man who has murdered can have that crime brushed under the carpet. It's television, radio and newspapers that mold our minds. And in this case, the media has done its job well. There are millions out there who believe that Bowman is a good man.

I will give these people credit. According to what they see and read about him I guess I would say the same thing, but they don't know the truth like I do. I just think that this is the best the Democratic Party had to offer, and instead of people knowing the truth, people will be led to believe the appearance and not the substance.

"I think I'm going to take a shower now, Baby."

I come out of my trance and see Jill walking toward the shower. My fixation on revenge and anger towards those who have wronged me, my family and my soon to be fiancé has taken a toll on me. My whole life looks as though I have lost my faith in those with power. It seems I get up every morning and all this hatred and anger flood back inside of me and instead of doing anything about it, I just sit back and let these disasters happen. The time has come for me to act and not sit back in despair and take it.

There goes Jill again and that karaoke imitation. Even with all the pent up anger I have, it's hard not to laugh at that awful singing. Mariah Carey eat your heart out. I should be used to this by now. She always does this in the shower. I get up and make my song bird a nice big pot of coffee. While filling the coffee maker, I think of what Jill and I could do today. It's time for me to just kick this anger and 'ability' crap to the curb for the day, or I will go absolutely crazy.

While the coffee brews and Jill gets done with her aria I scan the paper to see what is happening in this city of ours. I see an Arts Festival is going on downtown and that the new Pacino movie is showing. Jill will most likely want to go shopping, but I will throw out these ideas to Jill and hope one of them sticks. I don't feel like gallivanting through some mall while she looks at over priced clothes, although a stop by Victoria's Secret might warm my heart to the idea.

MOTION

    I can hear Jill zipping up in the bedroom. She comes out in her jeans and a thin sweater that matches her eyes perfectly. Heading for the coffee maker, Jill pours herself a full cup and asks me what I want to do today. After telling her, (and finding out I'm right about the shopping thing) she and I compromise a bit, decide on skipping the festival for a trip to the mall, and afterward, dinner and a movie. I wait patiently for an hour while Jill gets her load of caffeine and a jolt of SportsCenter before heading out.

9

Jill keeps going store to store searching for the perfect blouse. If there is a perfect blouse, I'm sure it isn't here in Indianapolis. I keep following her around like a puppy dog 'til I spot a bookstore out of the corner of my eye. After "getting Jill's permission," I head over and start browsing through the psych section.

There I find all sorts of interesting things. Ah, what do we have here? It's Judith Barksdale.... *Unimaginable*. Just flipping through the book, I see chapters on the mind's control over physical function and how there have been stories of such occurrences for over one hundred years. With what I have read in just five minutes, I realize this is what I need.

As I'm standing at the counter, I see Jill by the magazine rack flipping through the latest issue of *Cosmo* and *Glamour*.

"Jill, I found a bit of sanity today."

"What happened, Joel?"

"I found the book that I need!"

"It's about time, Babe, I thought you were going to go crazy pretty soon."

"How do you feel about going with me to Asheville, North Carolina?"

"What? Are you serious, Joel?"

"Why not? You have vacation time and so do I, plus there is no one else I'd rather go with."

"Just tell me when, sweetheart."

"Two weeks from now okay with you?"

"You bet, I'll let David know Monday."

With all the time I have put in at my job I'm sure I'll be able to get a week off. We leave after Jill glances through a few more magazines and we head out to a few more stores. Jill insists we stop by Victoria's Secret. I don't argue with her about it one bit. She asks me what colors I like when it comes to lingerie and I tell her, as I have so many times over the years, that I like black, red, white and sometimes a dark green. I've always said that Jill looks good in everything. I just find her to be naturally beautiful. After picking out a few things we head to the checkout, pay, and leave.

We get into the car and I suggest we go to a Mexican restaurant, Jill agrees. I pull the car into a parking space at El Tapatillo. The indication is that this is a great place with all the people standing outside the door. Jill and I walk past the crowd to one of the girls at the greeting counter. We ask how long the wait will be. She tells us about half an hour. I give her my last name and Jill and I head to the bar. Jill orders a glass of merlot and I just have a coke. We get into a discussion about getting married and she asks me if I looked for a ring yet.

"Yes, I have actually found one and put it on layaway."

"No way! What cut is it, size, how many diamonds, just the one diamond, or more than one?"

"Honey, you will love it. I found it in the fifth cracker jack box, so I saved some of that hundred bucks too."

Jill slaps me gently on the shoulder and smirks, and then a smile comes beaming from her. And I realize how lucky I am to have her in my life.

"What kind of gold, white or yellow?"

"Who said it was either? I do recall that only plastic comes in Cracker Jack boxes."

"Quit messing with me. I hate it when you don't tell me things that I am just dying to know."

"Well Jill, some things are better left as surprises. Just trust me when I say you will love the quarter carat diamondique I bought you."

After finishing our drinks and a few laughs, I glance over Jill's shoulder and see Ashley coming in with a guy. I didn't even know Ashley knew of this place. Jill sees me looking over her shoulder, turns around to see what caught my attention.

"Oh my gosh, Joel! That's David and Ashley! We've got to get out of here!"

"Just calm down, Jill. I'm sure there's a good explanation to this."

Before she can reply Jill's phone rings. It's her lawyer. She talks to her for a few minutes and hangs up, visibly shaken. She tells me that her lawyer contacted David and wanted to make a deal with him directly, before the gloves come off. Jill's lawyer gave him an option and he didn't take it. He's calling the bluff. Jill starts to panic with the news. Ashley has her back to us, so she doesn't see either of us and David is so into his conversation with Ashley that he doesn't notice us either.

Jill asks me to let her know if I can tell what's going on. I see that Ashley doesn't look too enthused about being there. She almost looks sick but I can't make out what David is saying to her. It doesn't look good though. His mannerisms make it look more as if he's firing her instead of going out to dinner and having a good time.

David definitely looks like the intimidating type. He's tall, boisterous, handsome (I guess), and very smart. His ego is starting to suffocate me and I ask Jill if we should just leave out the side door and go somewhere else. She insists we do and I pay for our drinks in cash. We scurry out the side door. Jill looks as though she's about to faint.

"What's wrong Babe?"

"Seeing Ashley with David makes me feel betrayed right now. She told me she was going to call her mother tonight and stay home."

"If it's any consolation Jill, she didn't look as though she wanted to be here tonight. I think your lawyer got to him and knows that you and Ashley are friends. He's just trying to scare her."

"What if she's been sleeping with him, Joel? I mean, I adore Ashley, but let's face it, she gets around."

"I know. I guess you should tell her you saw her here with him tonight and then just ask her point blank."

Jill sighs. "Let's just go home."

"Alright, just calm down a bit. For now, there is nothing to worry about. It's all speculation for now. We'll go, but just don't dwell on it right now, Okay?

"Okay."

We go home to my apartment this time. Jill can't stand the thought of staying at her place tonight, knowing that she may run into Ashley later. I can't blame her and I have to admit the possibility of Ashley and David did cross my mind the other day at dinner. When I told Ashley I was at the library and she said she hadn't seen me. Ashley knows my car and I was right in front of the library. She didn't even notice? It made me wonder and I'm wondering even more, but I don't want to tell Jill because I know it's all supposition on my part. I really do hope I am wrong.

I open the door to my apartment and Jill can't believe the filthy place she just walked into.

"My maid must have been on vacation these past two weeks."

"Who are you kidding? I'm your maid, Joel, and this is so disgusting."

There are pizza boxes open with pieces still in them from days before. Clothes are everywhere. Trash bags are staking a claim by the front door, and dishes are piled up in the sink.

"I need to take a shower Jill… you okay?"

She nods as I walk down the hall and enter the bathroom. I can hear her bagging trash and cleaning. My instincts are at work, and I can't help but smile. I knew Jill would start cleaning and this would make her forget temporarily, what happened tonight. It is something I have come to understand about her over the years. Jill worries about problems and her remedy is she needs something to keep her occupied, so she can forget for a while.

After getting cleaned up I head to my room. I hear the sink running in the kitchen as I walk down the hall. Once entering my room I realize I don't have any clothes to wear. They are all dirty and the only clean things I have are my socks and underwear. I put clean whites on and the cleanest jeans and t-shirt I can find and head back out to the kitchen area. I glance over to the sofa in the other room and I see Jill with her hands on her head, quietly sobbing. My therapy didn't work after all and now I was freaking out for her.

"What is wrong, Jill?"

"My world is coming apart, Joel. I was told the other day by David that I was expendable and could be replaced. I've had that on my mind and now my friend is with him and I don't know what's going on, or what to think. My dad is sick and if I tell him any of this he will go downhill. I can't take it Joel, you are all I have right now and I need you now more than ever."

I sit next to Jill, put my arm around her and kiss her gently on the forehead.

"Everything will be alright, I promise. I will always be here for you."

"Mike, could I get one?" I sit down at the bar and get ready to light a cigarette when I glance over and see drunken Jim a couple seats down from me. He gives me a soft wave to say hello right when Mike places a Blue Moon in front of me. My thoughts are running wild. I felt badly for leaving Jill at my place asleep, but I knew coming here would be good therapy for a few hours.

It's a good thing Jill fell asleep. Knowing the way she can't let go, I thought she would be up all night. I still can't believe Ashley showed up at the restaurant with David. Her being there with him has to do with Jill, but why is what Jill and I can't figure out. Knowing Ashley she will tell Jill what's going on eventually, but it is the not knowing that is hardest for her. I keep hoping that it is not be a big deal, but something deep inside seems that Ashley is hiding something. I just can't put my finger on it.

Jim slides down two seats from me and asks how I've been.

As soon as Jim asks, my cell phone rings and it just happens to be Jill.

"Joel, where did you go?"

"To Mike's."

"I got up and didn't see you and I got worried. Ashley called me and woke me up and I didn't see you here."

"I'm sorry, I needed to get out for a few to clear my head."

"Ash told me everything, Joel. David and Ash were sleeping together until I told her about the advances David made on me. Ash told me that when I told her about it, she called David to end their relationship and that she felt used."

"Why did they go to the restaurant together?"

"David wanted her back. That's what they were arguing about and she told him no way."

"Did you tell her that we were there?"

"I did and she felt guilty by not telling me about their affair sooner, but David just called her an hour before we saw them, to meet with her."

"Did David threaten her at all?"

"As a matter of fact, he did. He threatened her job if this ever got out and told her never to tell me. She said keeping it inside and me not knowing was to stressful. She said she needed to tell me before she lost her mind with the guilt."

"At least she does have a conscience. Are you going to be awake for a while?"

"I'm going to go back to bed. I just wanted to call and find out where you went and to tell you what Ash said."

"Thanks, Baby, it makes sense now. I'll be home in a little bit. I love you."

"I love you too Joel. Be safe."

Well, that answered a lot of questions I had. I am really starting to hate that scumbag David. I know Ashley slept with him because she felt her job was threatened. Then Jill told her what she was doing about the lawsuit. Because he didn't fire Jill, Ashley knew then that David wouldn't fire her, so she told him she wanted to end it and now he wants her back.

It all makes sense now and I do feel badly for Ashley, but she does get around. Ash did seem like she wasn't happy about being there when I saw her, but she gave in to his abusive, verbal charm long before tonight and now it is taking a toll on her. I ask Mike what I owed him and he slides the tab to me. After throwing some bills on the bar I walk out the back door and head home.

When I walk through the door, I see Ashley has come by. She and Jill are on the sofa talking. I can tell Ashley had been crying for a while. My first instinct is to go to the bedroom and just let them talk, but I am too curious about what Ashley might have to say, so I stay in the room with them. I ask both of them if they are bothered by me being there and they both say no.

Curious about what is to come, I ask Ashley if she's planning on quitting or sticking it out. She told us that she was thinking of moving back to her hometown of Columbus, Ohio, but that she wasn't sure yet.

Ashley leaves and as soon as the door shuts behind her, Jill starts telling me everything that happened between David and Ash. She tells me how Ash had been sleeping with David for years and how many times he threatened her job when she tried to end it. It is disgusting that a married man would sleep around like this, but even more disgusting that he would blackmail young women like this.

"Are you going to say anything about this to your lawyer Jill?"

"Only if I know she can use some of this info. Now I'm more afraid of Ashley's life being threatened than anything else. I didn't expect her to go into such detail about what David has done to her, but when she brought up that David has threatened her life tonight, I started feeling afraid for her."

"Well she brought this on herself. I agree that David has no right to threaten her, but Ash should never have put herself in that place to begin with."

Jill nods with agreement, but the emotion on her face tells me she is genuinely afraid for her friend Ashley. I don't know David that well, but if I base his character by what everyone tells me, I think he is the lowest scum on earth. The authorities should get involved, but with his connections to politics, mob and the Indy Police force, I'm afraid he could do something to someone and it getting swept under the carpet. He may go by the books when it comes to the court of law, but in his personal life he is as crooked as they come. I look over at Jill and she tells me she's going to bed. I kiss her goodnight and tell her I'll be in bed shortly.

I pick up the Barksdale book and read some more about stories that intrigue me and some stories which were from over a hundred years ago, about the condition I have. It would be nice to find someone on this earth who actually has this same 'ability'. My head hurts after reading for around half an hour.

11

The next evening, Ashley and Jill are at my apartment having a girl's night, while Nate and I go to the Pacer game. I pick up Nate and he seems a little nervous. After I ask him about our bet he tells me he quit his job. I ask him why and he tells me that when we get our winnings, the guys that place the bets want a ten percent cut. He tells me that the only way to make real money is to have him go to Las Vegas and place the bets for the both of us. I mention to him that all the winnings that I get I have to have cash.

Nate thinks about it a moment and says he can fly back to Indy every other week to get the winnings to me. He wonders how he can get that kind of money back to Indianapolis. I tell him just to mail it back in yellow cushioned envelopes so no one suspects anything, but that it must be sent in yellow envelopes, spread out during the week.

"What person am I going to drag to Conseco, to watch these games with me?"

"Take Jill, she loves the Pacers."

"Good point Nate, but how do we choose what games to see?"

"After this game we get tickets for the rest of the season and we bet every game. When you get to the games call me, so I can place the bet in Vegas and we should be good to go."

After talking to Nate for a few minutes I realize he is making sense. With the winnings we get, the bets we place over a certain amount, will be reported to the IRS. I still want cash for each game, so there are no electronic funds transferred. We talk some more about how we set up the cash flow and then he tells me he will call and let me know how it can work for both of us when he is out there.

Once we get inside the arena and get to our seats, he tells me that he has placed three bets. His bets placed were for the over-under, Pacers to win and Pacers to win the NBA Championship. Nate has been thorough with his betting skills and knows what he is doing, so I just let it go. I am convinced that Nate will do the job well. My only concern is that he may get into the drugs again. A couple years ago he was heavy into cocaine and heroin. If it weren't for some of his closest friends confronting him on it he never would have gone through rehab. Nate has been clean since, but I know it can be a lifelong battle. I hope he doesn't falter.

Well the game starts with a bad pass and the Pacers get an easy lay-up. It's becoming so easy, but I do feel emotionally drained after using my "talent" for a while. Nate leans over and tells me to save it till later.

"Don't blow it all in the beginning Joel!"

"I'm not, just testing it out to make sure it still works."

Nate leans over and smiles. Another pass out of bounds, a dribble off the side of the foot and a three point shot that goes over the backboard. I'm getting back into my rhythm.

At halftime the Pacers are up by fifteen and right on tempo. I'm starting to get the feel for my ability. If I spread the power throughout the game instead of all at once, I don't feel as tired. Nate looks down at his sheet for the bets he made and glances at me with that sheepish grin he has. I believe he is enjoying this circus I've created once more.

The Pacers come out and play well without my help and I don't even try a thing the third quarter. They are up by twenty six points and well on the way to getting the over on the game. To bet on the over, the points are set in Vegas that both teams combine for a certain amount of points. For example, if Vegas states that the game today with the Pacers has one hundred and eighty points, which means the teams have to score at least one hundred eighty points combined. This has already happened with the last bucket Miller made.

We reached the end of the game and the Pacers won by thirty five points. They did most of it themselves; with nothing like the circus I produced the last time Nate and I were here. Nate looks at me and tells me he wants to go to Manny's and talk over some things. I agree and we start to head out. As soon as we get out to the parking lot I tell him I need to call Jill for a moment and see how she is.

"Hey Baby, how are you?"

"I'm doing just fine. Ashley and I just finished drinking half a bottle of red wine and we were snooping through your things."

"What? I hope you're kidding!?"

"I am...Actually I saw that you had not washed your clothes in a while and took the liberty of doing a few loads for you. I hope you don't mind?"

"Why would I? You clean my apartment and do my laundry. You're awesome Jill."

"Am I going to see anything weird on SportsCenter tonight?"

"Not really, they didn't need my help too much tonight. Nate and I are going to Manny's. If you and Ash aren't toasted, why don't you come down here for a couple hours and join us."

"We might just do that. I'll call and let you know in, like, five minutes."

"OK, talk to you soon. I love you."

"Love you, too."

I tell Nate that Jill and Ashley might come. It will take them about half an hour after they decide. He nods and says, "It's cool." I always thought Ashley and Nate would make a good couple. Ashley is black, with fair skin. She has long dark hair, brown eyes and is very attractive. I know Nate will like her when he meets her tonight.

When we walk into Manny's the place is packed. I go to the bar and order a couple bottles while he tries to find a place for us to sit. As I turn he waves to me and I see him all the way in the back of the bar with a table. I head back and as soon as I put the bottles down my phone rings.

"Honey, Ash and I will be down shortly."

"OK, see you soon."

I tell Nate that Ashley is coming down and I tell him about her. He seems somewhat interested. Nate says he is looking forward to meeting her. He then mentions to me how much we won today.

It looks as though I made over forty grand and he made about fifteen hundred, but I remind him that he's getting a ten percent cut and he smiles. He tells me he forgot about that and hands me two tickets to the next game on Tuesday. Jill will love going, she has never turned down a chance to attend any event.

After talking to Nate for another fifteen minutes I look up

and see the girls heading towards our table. I introduced Nate to Ashley and they started to hit it off right away. Jill looks at me in amazement that they are getting along so well. Ignoring us, they keep talking, so I strike up a conversation with Jill.

"Guess what I have for Tuesday?"

"I don't know? What is it?"

"Two tickets to the game and one of them has your name on it."

"No way!! Nate doesn't want to go?"

"He asked me to take you. I thanked him and said that you would love it."

"I can't go, Joel. I promised Ashley I would go to that art exhibit on Tuesday after work."

Ashley and Nate are still talking. When there is a break in the conversation, Jill asks her about Tuesday and the game. Ashley turns to Nate and asks him to go with her and he replies with a, "yes". It looks as though Nate made a new friend and is interested in her just like I expected. I don't think Jill is too pleased because she is aware of Nate's past with the drugs and rehab and hasn't liked him since. She knows that Ashley would be good for someone like Nate, but doesn't mention it too much because she doesn't want her to get too close to Nate in case he would have a relapse.

After sitting and talking for an hour or so, Ashley and Nate exchange phone numbers and we all head back to my place. When we pull in and get out of our cars, I see Nate talk to Ashley for a moment and then Ashley hops into her car and leaves. I ask Nate why he was going to the arts festival with her when he told me he was going to Vegas and he told me he was postponing the trip till later in the week, after we rake in some cash and he can dig up some tickets for the rest of the season.

We keep discussing it while Jill walks into my apartment. Jill knew that this discussion was something she didn't want to hear. I tell Nate to wait for me in the car while I let Jill know I need to drop him off at home. She turns on the TV and nods when I tell her. I head right back out the door. When I drop Nate off I ask him when our winnings will be in and he assures me we should see some on Wednesday. I tell him to roll thirty grand and keep ten for me. He waves as I leave and then heads into his apartment.

12

    It's Monday morning and I have made a decision to quit my job, so I can spend more time investigating this ability of mine. I have been desirous in going to Asheville, North Carolina to meet with Judith Barksdale, but will not be able to if I keep this crazy job. I only work three twelve hour shifts, but to take the time I need, quitting is the only choice.

    Jill wakes up and comes out of the bedroom looking like she needs a couple more hours of sleep. I have her coffee ready and she pours a full cup. She sits down and notices that I have been thinking of something and asks me if I am up to something.

    "I'm quitting my job and doing some investigating."

    "It's your life Joel, do whatever you want. I'm not upset with it because I think you should see this woman to find out if there are any other cases like this."

    "Jill, I know you're disappointed, but I have plenty to live off of with what my parents left me. You know that I just used that job to keep me busy."

"I know. I'm not mad at you. I want you to find out more about this power you have. It will make you more at ease with everything."

"Thanks for understanding Jill."

When I go into work, I tell my supervisor Mr. Johnson I am leaving, take my personal things off my desk and split. I leave before anyone can say goodbye, or talk me into staying. My gut feeling was to quit, but it is kind of hard to leave a place that I have put five years of my life into.

As soon as I get out of the building I call Nate to meet me at Mike's Place around eleven. Nate tells me he received the money earlier than expected for the bets he made and wants to see me as soon as possible. He agrees to meet me at Mike's.

When I get to Mike's I look at the television as John turns it on. John is the daytime bartender at Mike's and is just as pleasant as Mike himself. I catch myself fixated on the television watching Senator Bowman and the anchorwoman telling the viewing audience that he is back in Indianapolis for a while until the Democratic Convention. She proceeds with her remarks mentioning that the Convention is in Chicago this year. I ask John for a coke and when he places it in front of me Nate walks in. As soon as Nate sits down, he plops a yellow business envelope on the table and says, "Here you go, buddy."

"Thanks Nate. Did you take your cut and roll it over?"

"I sure did, Joel, and you know what? My bet for the Pacers to win the NBA Championship couldn't be placed, so they rolled that into our Pacers to win bet and we hit big. There is twenty grand in the envelope and whatever you don't need let me know and I'll roll it."

"Thanks Nate, I am picking up a ring for Jill today with this money and asking her to marry me while we are in North Carolina this coming weekend."

"I'll go with you to pick it up now if you want. I want to see this rock you bought her."

"Sounds good, let's go."

I throw some bills on the bar and tell John thanks. Nate and I head out the front door of the bar, hop into my car and take off down to the jeweler. My nerves are getting the best of me and having Nate come with me will relieve some of that. Nate and I talk about the games this week and when he expects to go to Vegas. He tells me that Jill and I have to go to the Tuesday, Thursday and Friday games, so we can get some sort of cash flow going. I agree unreservedly and tell him I quit my job today.

"What are you thinking Joel?"

"I just feel I need to spend more time with this and not that dead end job."

"That's cool, but what is the deal with going to North Carolina?"

"Jill has no idea, but I want to propose at the Biltmore."

"Very nice, I know she will like that, you stud. Well, when you get back I should be in Vegas setting up shop. Just call me so we can get the ball rolling on this betting thing."

"That won't be a problem. I'm into this just as much as you are, Nate, but I have to ask Jill to marry me this weekend. I want to have this done because I've procrastinated too long in asking her to be my wife. We need to have very little distractions when we start this betting thing."

"I agree, my man."

We pull into the same parking spot I was in when going to the library the other day. I take about four grand out of the envelope and we head to the jeweler.

"I've come to pick up a ring and here's my ticket."

Mr. Jones who helped me with the ring comes from the

back, takes the ticket from the girl helping us, finds the ring and brings it to the counter. He tells me that he had the ring sized to my liking and he opens the case it is in and it is beautiful. Nate looks in amazement when he sees it and says:

"Joel, if this girl doesn't marry you I will. That ring is gorgeous."

When Nate makes that comment we all hear the front door open and it is Ashley. She comes to the counter to ask us what we are doing there and sees the ring on the counter. Her face illuminates as she finally comprehends what is going on. "Joel, is this for Jill?"

"It sure is, Ashley, and if you say a word to her, I will have you put in a shallow grave."

"Don't worry about that. When do you plan to ask her?"

"This weekend in North Carolina, when we are on vacation. She was trying to get the following week off to hang at home, but I guess David wanted her to go this coming week because you weren't busy in the office. She has no clue about what kind of trip she's going on. By the way, how did you know we were here?'"

"I was leaving the library and walked out the front door when I saw your car pull up. My curiosity brought me into the store and I just had to find out what you had up your sleeve."

"Do you like the ring, Ash?"

"It is so Jill. Joel, she is going to love it."

I keep looking at the ring and finally Mr. Jones asks me if I have another payment for it. When I tell him I want to pay cash in full his eyes perk up and I slowly count it to him, one hundred dollar bill after one hundred dollar bill. After I pay, I put the ring in my pocket and head out the door with the two love birds talking to each other on our way out.

It's good to see Nate with a girl he can have a good time with.

I overhear the conversation and notice that they are planning on going out tonight. Nate gets a soft kiss on the cheek as Ashley takes off back to the office. I remind her not to say a word to Jill and she giggles as she walks away. When she is out of sight, I feel it necessary to bust Nate's chops.

"Where are you taking your new friend tonight?"

"I thought a dinner and a movie makes a classic first date."

"You know Nate, her ex-boyfriend used to be a lineman for the Colts a few years ago. He is a jealous man that does stalk her on occasion. I heard he beat the crap out of a boyfriend she had."

Nate just looks at me in disbelief and he just stares at me. I can't hold my laughter in anymore and tell him, "She never dated a guy from the Colts, I was just kidding. I made the story up."

"I'm going to get you back, Warner, you watch."

I start laughing at him as we get back into the car and drive away.

The next morning Nate calls me and tells me he enjoyed being on a date for the first time in a long time. His last was with Kelly, it seems so long ago and to this day he still wonders if she loved him for himself, or for the drugs he always provided for her. He still wonders how she is doing, or if she deteriorated more on the drugs. Because it has been such a long time, Nate was nervous and really wanted to make a good impression to Ashley.

He picked Ashley up at her place and she looked great as always. She wore a little black dress that revealed her gorgeous body. She wore her hair down and curled. After opening and closing the car door for her, he hopped into the driver side and they took off to a popular French restaurant on Clark Street.

Upon entering the restaurant, Nate mentions to the hostess that he has reservations for two. She finds his name in the reservation book and escorts them both to their table. After settling in, Ashley and Nate start talking about where they came from and how they both ended up in Indianapolis.

She tells Nate that she grew up in Columbus, Ohio and attended Ohio State where she graduated with a Political Science Masters Degree. Her story moves on to where she moved to Indianapolis for some guy that broke her heart a few years ago, and if it were not for Jill and I she would have moved back to Columbus long ago. She goes into great detail as to why she treasures Jill's friendship and how much they have both gone through together.

Nate starts talking about his upbringing in Minnesota and how his parents moved the family to Indianapolis. His father ended up getting a job here and he ended up liking it in Indianapolis after high school and stayed. He tells her that he did get into drugs heavily and that I helped him through it. After telling her that he has been sober and off the drugs for a couple years now, she breathes a sigh of relief. Once they order their food they both talk about Jill and I, how we both have been good friends and celebrate their fondness of us by toasting some champagne.

Ashley asks Nate why they are at such a fancy restaurant and he replies he wanted it to be the perfect first date. She smiles and sips some more of her champagne and then just looks into Nates' eyes. He looks into her eyes and they both share the rest of the night telling more stories, mostly stories of how much Jill and I have meant so much to both of them.

Nate finally winds up his conversation about the happenings of the night.

"Joel, this girl is incredible. She was so into everything I said and wants to go out again."

"I'm so glad everything went well. Jill and I were hoping you two would get along since you both are very close to us."

"I also wanted to tell you that even though it will be hard, I'll go to Vegas for a month or so to get our plan going. I am really into Ashley and want to keep seeing her."

"Just don't get ahead of yourself, Nate. It's only been one date, you know."

"I know, but I just feel so at ease with her. She is so attractive, but I feel like I can tell her anything. I told her about how you were there for me when I had the drug problem and that's probably one of my biggest secrets. Even after telling her that, she still seemed very interested in me."

"I'm happy things went well Nate, give me a call before my trip. I have some things I need to discuss with you."

"OK, brother, will do."

As soon as I hang up the phone with Nate, Ashley knocks on the door and Jill answers with anticipation. She comes in with a huge smile on her face and tells both of us how great her date went. Her conversation with Jill was almost making me wonder if she went out with Nate or some other guy. The man she is describing is nothing what I expected out of him.

Nate opened and closed doors for her and complemented the way she looked. She mentioned that since Jill and I were such good friends that they spent most of the evening talking about us. After about fifteen minutes of talking about her date, she says she has to get up early for work, and exits to her apartment.

It's a beautiful sunny day and Jill heads to work. Since I don't have to be at work today, I can do some more reading on the Barksdale book and find out some more information. I can't believe that Jill and I are going to North Carolina this weekend and I still don't know where this Judith Barksdale lives. My interest is growing as I flip through the pages of her book. She talks about many cases of telekinesis and how her studies showed that most of her subjects didn't exhibit any side effects, like drowsiness or exhaustion, like I do.

My curiosity is running wild and I start to call information to retrieve a phone number, so I can contact Judith. After about an hour of calling around the entire city of Asheville, I finally did get a number, but am too nervous to call it. I call a hotel close to the Biltmore and set up a reservation, drink a cup of coffee. Then settle down when I call the number.

"Hello is Judith Barksdale there."

"Speaking."

"My name is Joel and I have been reading some of your books. I wanted to tell you not only that I enjoy reading them, but may have a condition that I hope you can shed some light on."

"You have peaked my interest, Joel. What condition do you think you have?"

"I don't like telling too many people my condition, but I have the ability to make people physically do things just by thinking about it."

"I'm glad you called, Joel. I would be happy to hear more about this condition you have. My time is limited today, but I would love to hear more about this. Joel, from now on call me, Judy. I hate it when people call me Judith. It sounds too formal to me."

"Alright Judy, will do. It's funny you say that because I was hoping to make a trip to Asheville this weekend to meet you."

Judy invites me to meet with her when I am in town so she can learn more about my ability. I ask Judy about bringing Jill with me because I want to ask for Jill's hand in marriage at the Biltmore Mansion. She tells me that she has some connections there to make it a more romantic event.

I tell her that I am interested in learning about others dealing with the same ability that I have. Judy ends our conversation by saying that she knows one man that does, but that he doesn't like to talk about it and he is somewhat of a hermit. After giving me her address and a welcome invitation, she ends the conversation and I feel so much better now than I have in two weeks.

It is Friday and I do have a game tonight, but now that I know Judy is willing to see me, I feel more at ease. My senses are running wild and I think about any loose ends I need to tie up before heading to tobacco road. Nate is the first that comes to mind and while I have a moment, I call him on his cell phone.

"Hey buddy, what's up?"

"I just wanted to call and see how we've done so far this week."

"I want to stop by before your trip and give you some of your winnings. We hit big by the way and I will fill you in when I see you."

"Nate, I have to stop by my place and pack some things before leaving for this weekend. Why don't you just meet me there?"

"Sounds good, my man. I'll be there around six. Is that OK with you?"

"That sounds great, see you then."

After reading Judy's book for another hour, I check the clock and it is almost time for my Jill to come home. It's about 5:30 p.m. and I want to tell her about packing and getting some things from my apartment before we go to the game tonight. The game starts at eight, so we have to leave here by seven, so we can be there at tip off.

It's not necessary since I could get there in the fourth quarter and still dictate the end of the game. Once I hear Jill's car pull in, I head out the door and meet her in front of the apartment. I tell her that I need to get a few things and should be back by seven. I kiss her and drive over to my apartment where Nate is parked, waiting for me.

I talk to Nate about his flight in the morning to Vegas and he tells me that Ashley is taking him to the airport. Once inside my apartment, he keeps telling me his plan of doing a lot of betting and finding out the best ways to handle such huge bets. He tells me that I have made over two hundred thousand dollars this week alone and he hands me a few yellow envelopes.

I see the huge bulge in both of them. I look at Nate and he tells me there is twenty five thousand in each envelope and that he is rolling one hundred fifty for me. My heart races a bit when I open one of the envelopes and I see all the one hundred dollar bills in it.

I ask Nate how much he has made himself and he tells me that he has five thousand in cash and ten thousand rolled. I take about ten thousand out of the envelope I just opened and I give it to him, trying to thank him for his part in all this. He refuses, but I tell Nate it is for him getting comfortable out in Vegas, so he can concentrate on the business at hand. I tell him if he wants to bet the money he can, if he doesn't, then it's his to spend.

Nate tells me that once we win, he will be able to get the cash immediately and doesn't have to wait for it. We both talk some more as I pack and when I am done, we both head out my front door. It's a good thing Nate is here because he reminded me to pack the ring in my bag. After running back in to get it and packing it away, I wish Nate the best and head back to Jill's apartment.

It is 6:45 p.m. and I realize I got back earlier than I expected. Jill opens the door with a toothbrush in her mouth. I tell her that Nate is getting a ride to the airport from Ashley in the morning, and she gives me a thumbs-up sign while brushing her teeth. After she finishes, she comes out and tells me that Ashley already told her that, while at work. I ask Jill if she's ready and we head out the front door.

Once Jill and I get to the field house, we realize that we missed a little bit of the first quarter. She tells me that we have to stop by the food stand because she's starving. I hand the tickets to the usher and when we get inside, we dash to the nearest vendor. After getting a couple of cokes and hotdogs we head in and see that the Pacers are up by three with five minutes to go until the end of the first quarter. Jill and I take our seats and we start eating, with a coke in one hand and a couple hotdogs in the other. I realize this eating thing could be a little complicated.

When we finish eating I realize that the Pacers may not need my help. They are up by six at the end of the first quarter, and when I talked to Nate earlier in the day, I told him just to bet on the Pacers to win. He told me that the Pacers were favored by four, so I need to make sure they maintain this lead. Jill looks over at me and starts talking about our trip to North Carolina. She asks me if we are stopping anywhere to spend the night.

I told her I want to drive after the game because we won't hit any traffic. She likes that idea, and tells me that she can't wait to get down there because she heard that Asheville is one of the most beautiful places during the spring. I tell her that since we are already there, we could do some traveling down to Myrtle Beach, Charleston and Savannah if she wants.

After talking to her for a few minutes, I see that the Pacers extend their lead to twelve with four minutes to go until half. I start getting excited because I may not have to use this ability tonight if they keep this up. Jill looks at me and asks if I have done anything yet and I just shake my head and smile. She starts talking about the trip again and by this time I wonder if Ashley told her about the ring. Jill keeps talking about the trip like she is trying to squeeze some information out of me. She doesn't know that the more she tries, the more resistant I will be in spilling any knowledge.

I look up and the Pacers are up by fifteen at half, I ask Jill if she is still hungry and if she wants anything more. She nods and says she is still hungry. I tell her to wait and I run down the steps and head down the tunnel to the nearest food vendor before the longer lines start forming from the halftime rush. While I was waiting in line I give Nate a quick call and talk to him for a minute.

"I haven't done a thing tonight, Nate! They seem to be doing alright without me! What are you up to?"

"Just finishing my packing and getting everything ready for a long week in Vegas."

"I feel so bad for you, Nate."

"Have you heard from Ashley tonight? I tried calling her and it keeps going straight to her voicemail."

"I wouldn't worry about her. She usually spends Friday nights with her girlfriends. She'll probably call you later since she's taking you to the airport tomorrow."

"Yeah, I just thought she would want to hang since it will be my last day here for a while."

"Just call her later… she will be up late. Jill and I are taking off to North Carolina after the game, so good luck to ya. I'll call you when we get back."

"OK, let me know when you get back into town and we'll get this betting machine going again."

"No problem, have a safe trip, Nate."

"You too my man, and take care."

As soon as I end the call it is my turn in line. The lady asks for my order and this time I just order three hotdogs and a soft pretzel. She quickly brings the food and rings me up in record time. I head into the arena and I see Jill with a concerned look on her face. She tells me that she just tried to call Ashley and she didn't answer her phone, that it went straight to voicemail. I tell her that I just got off the phone with Nate, he told me that he tried to call her and the same thing happened. After reassuring Jill that she is fine, I tell her that Ashley probably didn't realize she turned off her cell phone. Jill takes a couple hotdogs, eats them plain and chases them down with a slurp of coke.

When the fourth quarter starts, the Pacers extend their lead to twenty three and are in control of this game. They are playing Memphis, so it shouldn't be hard for the Pacers to put them away. I see that the game is under control and ask Jill if she has everything packed. She nods her head while taking another sip from her coke, then asks me if I have done anything yet. My answer is still no, and then I ask her if she feels like driving tonight and she tells me yes, as long as I am the one driving first so she can sleep.

As the game gets to the last minute, the Pacers are up by seventeen and look as though they will win this by four very easily. I grab Jill's hand and ask her if she is ready and we take off down the tunnel and head out the main entrance. There is no one around us as we jog through the parking lot to my car. We take off to Jill's to get her things before we start our excursion to North Carolina.

15

We are on our way. Jill is asleep, but all I can think about is how Judy is going to react when I show her my ability. I keep wondering how I can show her without doing any harm. My mind keeps dwelling on this as I keep driving, trying to get my mind off of this as I turn on the radio with hope of hearing some news. My soon to be fiancé is squirming around on the passenger side trying to get comfortable. She wakes up for a brief moment and asks me, "Do you have any idea where we are?"

"We are in Alaska somewhere. I just saw a moose, but didn't want to wake you."

"Not funny, Joel, I don't want to hurt you."

"We are in the lovely state of West Virginia my dear. Ever see the movie Deliverance?"

Jill thinks for a moment and says, "Is that the one where Ned Beatty…"

"Yes it is and we are in the southern part of the state where that kind of thing could possibly occur."

"Then quit talking to me, and get us out of this state."

My sick sense of humor has bored her to sleep once again. I keep listening to the radio and hear the sports headlines. He runs down the scores of the NBA games and I hear him say the Pacers lost.

"The Pacers lost?"

He quickly corrects himself and says the Pacers won by thirteen. I almost have a heart attack and with my loud outburst she wakes up and hits my arm in disgust. It finally hits Jill what I screamed out, and she freaks for a moment. Her look is priceless and I finally tell her that the newsman corrected himself.

"The Pacers won by thirteen honey, go back to sleep."

She plops her head back down on the pillow she brought. I guess I deserve that smack on the arm since I have been very sarcastic lately. Just when I think Jill is back to sleep, she startles me a bit and asks me if I am OK to drive, and I tell her that I am fine.

"Since we're out of West Virginia Joel; why don't we stop for coffee? I could use some."

"That sounds good. I'll look for a place."

I keep driving for another half hour and see that there is a Starbucks off the next exit. It is around 5:30 a.m. and I have my doubts they are open, but we can always drink the rot gut gas station coffee if they aren't. After pulling off the exit and stopping by the Starbucks, I do see that they will open soon. There is a gas station down the street and I head there to get a newspaper. When I get the paper and come back to the car I notice Jill is wide awake.

We head back to the Starbucks and get some freshly made coffee. As Jill heads to the bathroom, I sit down and start reading the paper. It's my wonderful friend Senator Bowman on the cover again. This time to my amazement the story isn't good and has a picture of some girl, next to his, claiming the Senator impregnated her. When Jill comes out of the bathroom and sits down I show her the front page and she is stunned that the press waited this long to put out the scoop. She reads the story while I head to my favorite... the Sports section. I read about the NBA, baseball scores and tell Jill the Reds won, behind Jackson's three hitter.

After reading the paper and downing a couple cups of coffee, Jill and I hit the road again. Jill intends on talking to me the entire rest of the trip. She tells me that the article on Bowman said that the girl who accused him has a history of lying and making false claims. I didn't have to hear this because I knew it would happen. It kind of reminds me of the Clinton-Flowers ordeal. Gennifer Flowers came out providing audio tapes to the media, with Clinton leaving messages to her, and admitted an adulterous affair with him, but none of the media pursued it.

I am not saying I am a Republican, by any means. My view is that all politicians are crooked and that is why I am registered Independent. The faith and hope I once had for my politicians went out the window when one of them killed my parents because he was driving drunk. It isn't necessarily all Bowman and his irresponsibility, but the media and judicial system. I still to this day, don't understand how he could get away with killing and not serve any time in prison whatsoever.

It is a travesty to see how he came out of that unscathed and caused a poor teenager like me to not have a family anymore. Nobody in the media picked up on this, and I'll bet if you asked a majority of people in Indianapolis if they remember what happened to me, they wouldn't have a clue. I guess the message that I am getting at is that politicians are untouchable and they all know it. We the people of this country have to abide by the rules and laws, but they can twist them and have judges and media moguls do favors for them that make them appear morally sterile.

After going through this rant in my head, I tune into what Jill is talking to me about. She keeps going on and on about Ashley and why she never called Jill back. I ask her to just call her from the cell phone, but she declines saying that it's still too early. Nate leaves this morning and I hope Ashley takes him, but my heart is saying that she might forget. I don't mention my fears to tell Jill, because I know she will worry more.

We keep talking for the next couple of hours and I see that we are close to Asheville. I take a folded sheet of paper with Judy's address out of my front pocket and hand it to Jill and ask her to hold on to that 'til we get to the city limits. Once there, I ask her what the address is and she tells me. I keep remembering what Judy told me about the directions to her house. After getting lost for about five minutes, we pull up to her humble Cape Cod style home. It is a beautiful dwelling, with a majority of her perennials blooming in the flower beds.

Jill sits in the car as I casually walk to Judy's front door and knock. A few seconds go by and I knock again. I keep thinking to myself that I should have called her when we arrived into town, but I am already here. While I start walking back to the car, I hear the front door open and as I turn around, a woman that looks like Meryl Streep answers the door.

"You must be Joel! I'm so excited to finally meet you!"

"Why, thank you, Judy. You seem to be more excited about meeting me than I am nervous about meeting you."

"Nervous? Please, I always enjoy company when they could be a potential client."

"I didn't know I was a possible client?"

"You aren't, I was just kidding. I haven't practiced in years. Where is this lovely girl you told me about?"

I waved at Jill to come up and as she gets out of the car and Judy comments on how beautiful she is. After introductions, Judy gives us a small tour of her home.

Once Jill and I get settled, Judy asks me to come enter her make shift office on the second floor. She asks Jill to watch TV and make herself at home. Judy leads me into her office and when she follows me in, she closes the door. I tell her that I am tired and although I would like to bear my soul to her, I just can't get the strength, but she insists that it is about my proposal to Jill.

She has a friend that works at the Biltmore and she tells me that he will have something special for the both of us out in back of the Biltmore estate, by the huge garden. Judy states that his name is Paul and that he owes her big, so if there are any screw-ups to let her know. She states that we are supposed to do it Sunday afternoon around 3:00 p.m.

Judy asks me if I could share a little about my ability and I tell her that I can give her a demonstration. I ask her to sit behind her desk, and I see that she has a pen and pencil holder toward the front of her desk. Judy walks behind her desk to sit down.

When she gets settled, I ask her to pick up the holder, grip it comfortably in her hand and lift it off the table.

She does so willingly and asks me what to do now. I tell her that I will make her drop it without her wanting to. She smiles and tells me to try; within a second, she drops it and the pens and pencils that were once in the holder are now all over her desk. It was quite jovial, but it was the safest way to show her my curse.

After pondering this moment in time, Judy looks me in the eyes and asks me if I have been the one responsible for the Pacers winning streak. I ask her how she would know something like that. She responds with the fact that I do live in Indianapolis, that she is a huge sports fanatic, and she just put two and two together. I nod my head yes while she asks me how much I have in my bank account due to the Pacers. She laughs, saying she is kidding.

"How much you have in your bank account is none of my concern, Joel."

Judy tells me that she has heard of cases where a documented few people over the last thousand years have had this power. I keep telling her of wanting to find someone with this ability, so I can have someone to converse with about moral decisions in using this power. Her questions deepen as she asks me what kind of moral judgments I would inquire about. She tells me something that I'm sure will make me think deeply:

"Joel, did you ever see the serial killer, or a man that was a mass murderer interviewed and say they didn't feel like they could do such a horrendous thing. They felt as though someone took over their body and felt as though they couldn't control themselves. Who's to say that someone may have the same power as you and made them do something like that?"

"I didn't imagine it would be that profound, but I guess it

could happen. When I stop to think about it, only a few people know of this power I have, so it's not like a world wide fact that I have this power. I guess someone could possess it and not tell anyone and make people do things they wouldn't do on a normal basis."

"You see Joel, your gift is just that… a gift. To have a gift like this and to rationalize it in a moral sense is very rare. Most of my studies have indicated that the ones that do have this power that no one knows about causes them to do things that are selfish which brings out the greed inside them. This means that you have found your responsibility with this power. Now that you know the moral standing behind it, you shouldn't beat yourself up with rationalizing it. Your convictions on how it must be used, is enough to keep you from creating evil with it. I do want to leave you with a question that you have time to answer. How can you justify using your power for good if you have already let bad dictate your power already? I just want you to think what damage you have already done by throwing games and involving a friend of yours into this web of greed you created."

We talk for a few more minutes, I tell her that I need to rest because my eyes are about to sink into my head. I keep thinking about what she has just said and I do feel more at ease, but guilty for getting Nate involved in all of this. It is good to finally get some insight on this gift I have and in the way I should use it. My thoughts wonder toward doing something that I may think is for the greater good, but how someone observing my action may think it is evil. I let it go for now, so I don't spend time telling Judy my deepest feelings on the issue and end up falling asleep while trying to listen to her incredible wisdom on the subject.

Judy and I leave her office and head downstairs to check on

Jill. She fell asleep on the sofa with the remote for the TV still in hand. I end up sitting next to her and Judy asks me if I would like anything to drink or eat, and I shake my head no. She offers for us to stay at her place. I try to refuse, but she insists we stay with her. My call to the hotel is brief, when I cancel the reservation.

I follow up by asking her if she might have a pillow I could rest my head on. She asks me if I would like to sleep in the guest room. After waking Jill, she and I head back to the guest room and fall asleep on the bed immediately.

After checking my watch and seeing that I had seven hours of sleep, I sit up in bed to the smell of a heavenly meal Judy must be making. I glance over and see that Jill isn't in bed anymore and I straggle out to the kitchen where I see both of them talking and cooking something exquisite. While plopping myself down on a kitchen chair Jill turns, walks over smiling, kisses me and asks if I had a good sleep. While I nod my head yes, Judy informs me what we are having for dinner. She tells us it is fried chicken, green beans, mashed potatoes, rolls and chocolate cake for dessert.

As I start to drool I ask Judy if she would mind if I went out front to smoke a cigarette. She asks me if I would like some company and asks Jill to stir the green beans. We both head out the front door. While smoking she tells me that she absolutely adores Jill. I ask her how long she talked to her while I was asleep and she replies:

"About two hours, she speaks so fondly of you Joel. Jill told me how you both met when you were kids and how you started dating. It was all so very refreshing to hear the true romance that you both share."

"Jill is the greatest woman I know. I don't know what I would do without her. She keeps my head out of the clouds when I feel that I am helpless and there's no hope. Jill was so great to me after my parents died and was always there when I doubted my faith."

"So you're a religious one, Joel."

"I wouldn't say that now. I've experienced things in life that have definitely made me wonder why God lets bad things happen to good people. Even after the events in my life, I never doubted my belief in God, but always wondered how experiences that are so tragic could have a silver lining, and she kept me focused on what was right. What can I say, she's my best friend."

"You seem to be very lucky Joel. I wish both of you the best."

"Thanks Judy, I want to thank you for putting us up these next few days. It is a gracious gesture that is greatly appreciated."

Judy and I keep talking until Jill comes out and tells us that dinner is about ready. After eating and cleaning up afterward, we sit in Judy's' family room and discussed our life experiences. I come to realize that Judy was a brilliant person that worked hard throughout her life to what she has become now.

She has spent years of trying to please her parents in the field she decided to go into and the men she seemed to compete with in her field, just to be respected by her peers. I did ask her why she retired at such a young age and her response was that she was just burned out on the competition men always seemed to have with her. Judy went into detail and I couldn't believe what some of her bosses did as well as men she worked with.

Jill followed up with her dilemma at work and what she was pursuing. It just so happened that Judy knew who David Johns is and said she was hired to do a psychological profile for someone David Johns was defending. She told us that the case was from the early 1980's, but does remember David being a very controlling attorney. Her description of David is exactly what everyone says about him. Judy then tells Jill that with the evidence she claims to have on David that she should try and settle.

"If this goes to court Jill, you will be put under a microscope. Your credibility will be on the line and people will find a way of disliking you. It will not be because of the media, but what this firm will do to defend its own boss. They will be like vultures and say terrible things about you and try to break you emotionally and physically. Just be careful in what you say and do."

When Judy is done telling Jill how to prepare for her case if it goes to court, Jill's mobile phone rings and it is Ashley. Their conversation pierces the quiet evening and I can hear every word.

"Where have you been Ash?!"

"I slept over at a girlfriend's house, but I woke up in time to get Nate to the airport. I'm so sorry I didn't get back to you sooner, I turned my phone off and accidentally left it at home when I went out last night."

"I'm just glad you're OK."

"I wanted to see if you had a safe trip and to let you know I was alright."

"We had a good trip, but I slept a majority of the way here. How was Nate when you dropped him off at the airport?"

"He was good and he wanted me to come out to Vegas in a few weeks, but we'll see."

"I'll call you soon Ash, take care."

"You too Jill, have fun."

All three of us talk for a while longer. When we see that it is becoming very late we all retire to our bedrooms.

17

I wake up and it is a beautiful Sunday morning. The birds are singing and it is a bright sunny day with not one cloud in the sky. While slipping out of the bed and not waking Jill, I step out to the front porch and see Judy sitting on her porch swing smoking a cigarette from one hand and a huge cup of coffee in the other. She asked me if I slept well, and if I wanted to bum a smoke off of her. I nod my head yes, take the smoke from her pack on the table, and light up. Judy tells me there is coffee in the kitchen and cream and sugar next to the coffee maker. I go in and grab a cup and realize it is Kona Coffee which Jill will absolutely love.

When I arrive back outside Judy asks me when I planned on heading up to the Biltmore. I tell her that we will leave around 2:00 p.m. After calling her friend Paul and telling him when we will arrive she tells me that Paul has arranged a seating for both of us in the garden. He will have champagne ready and a blanket thrown over one of the benches when we arrive.

She then asks me to tell about Jill and what she thinks of this power I have. I tell her that Jill has always treated me the same and that I have often wondered if she has known for a long time that I had this power. The way she treats me now is no different than before, but I know deep down Jill knew I had this ability before I proved it to her. Judy asks me why and how I knew this.

"Her feelings for me never wavered and she never asked me a million questions like I anticipated."

"Did you ever ask her why she never did?"

"No, especially now that she has this lawsuit on her mind, I don't want to disrupt her concentration on the case."

"You have to ask Joel, just for peace of mind."

"I know, I have wondered that myself, but I am afraid there might be an incident that she remembers from some time ago, where she may have thought that I was different from anyone else she has known."

Judy and I talk for a few more minutes and Jill walks out the front door and wishes us both a good morning. While Judy mentions to her there is coffee already brewed in the kitchen, Jill wraps her arms around me, kisses my cheek and heads back in to get some coffee. When Jill comes back out I ask her a question about my power and if she knew that I was different a long time ago.

She asks me if I remember a bully from when we were kids, whose name is Scott Davis. I think about it for a moment and then it does hit me. I remember that clown. He was terrible to Jill.

"Do you remember when he attacked me one time and you stood in front of him and he went to hit you?"

"I do remember that, but he never hit me."

"I know, because when he threw the punch his fist came flying at you and right when it was an inch from your face, it was like he stopped, but not on his own. It felt as though you had some sort of force field surrounding you and he could not penetrate it."

"Now it's all becoming clear, Jill."

"Joel, from that instant, I knew you were different and I started to realize there was something special about you from that moment. You were going to take a punch for me and you had no idea at the time he would freeze up like that. I could tell, because you shook like a leaf afterward, but I wondered then if you had a special power."

Jill tells me of some instances other than that one, but none that affected her like the one Scott Davis is known for doing. We keep talking and she knew back then I would figure out what my power was one day, but she thought I knew about it long before a month ago. While observing both of us, Judy tells us how great a couple we are. She can visually see the respect and love we have for each other. After a morning of reading the paper and sharing stories, Jill and I get ready to drive to the Biltmore for our memorable day together.

Jill and I walk towards the front of the Biltmore where a gentleman in a tuxedo comes and introduces himself as Paul. My amazement starts when I try to figure out how Paul knows who we are. Without interrupting him, we follow him where he leads us to the back of the mansion which happens to have a huge garden with paths zigzagging through it.

He takes us to a bench which at this time I can tell is made out of cement or marble, but the closer we get to it I realize it is covered with a velvet looking blanket and two champagne glasses and an unmarked bottle in a bucket of ice. Once we arrive he seats us at the bench and he briskly walks away. When we sit down, Jill looks at me in amazement and asks me what is going on. While stunned her eyes move with mine as I shift from the bench to one knee on the pathway.

"Jill I am sure you didn't expect this to happen today, but I am here right now to ask you for your hand in marriage."

When I pull out the ring from my pocket, I see Jill start to tear up.

"You have made me so happy throughout the years we have known each other and I want that same happiness for the rest of my life. Jill Zoeller, will you marry me?"

Without hesitation she answers with an emphatic:

"Yes, did you have any doubt?"

As I slide the ring on her finger, people that had gathered around us in the garden start to applaud. Since we are both shy in public gatherings as it is, we simply blush on cue. After I give Jill a hug and kiss we both sit back down on the bench. I start to pour what looks like champagne into the glasses as she slides her new ring back and forth on her finger, trying to get every sparkle from the reflection of the sun. When I ask her if she had any clue she takes a sip and says:

"I had no clue you would do this. My mind is racing right now, so I am not thinking straight. Who do you know down here that would set this up?"

"Judy, she was excited to do this for us. She seems like a very romantic person at heart."

When I mention this, Paul comes up and tells us that since he didn't know if we drink alcohol, he placed a bottle of sparkling cider in the bucket of ice and wishes both of us a happy and fruitful life together. I thank him and he walks away. Jill is staring at me in amazement as she takes another sip, then radiates a smile and asks me if anyone knew this is happening today.

"Nate and Ashley knew, but your parents didn't know. Now that I think of it maybe I should have requested your dad's blessing."

"My dad has a heart condition Joel, I'm glad you didn't! Give me your cell phone so I can call them. I didn't bring mine with me today."

"Hey Babe, remember your dad has a heart condition. I don't think it would be such a good idea."

I just chuckle a little as she snatches my phone away from

me and calls her parents. She tells them the great news. Although I am sitting three feet away I can hear her mom happily screaming. Jill tells me everything her mom is saying to her. Jill's mom tells her that Jill's sisters came over to the house after church and wondered if we were ever going to get married.

After we go through speaking to each one of Jill's family members and all of them congratulating us, we head toward the front of the mansion and take the tour. I can't help but see how happy Jill is just by looking at her beaming smile. My mind isn't even focused on the tour we are taking and I tune in to her and how she makes me feel. Jill leans over and whispers to me that she has never been happier in her life than she is right now.

We leave the Biltmore with both of us not having a recollection of doing so. Neither one of us paid attention to the tour guide, so I picked up a book about it from the gift shop and we left a happy couple. Once we get back to Judy's home, we both see her sitting on the swing in the front and she waves with excitement. She heads over to Jill's side and as soon as Jill gets out of the car, Judy asks her if she could see the ring.

Judy takes one look at it and states how beautiful it is. After going through the details of the entire afternoon with Judy, I mention a thank you for all that she did to arrange it. I tell her that Paul did a wonderful job of setting it up, and that the cider was a nice touch. Judy asks us to come inside because she cooked us dinner again.

While sitting on the sofa Judy talks loudly from the kitchen on how she enjoys cooking, especially when guests come over. She proceeds to tell us how happy she is for the both of us, asks when the wedding date will be and other questions that Jill and I haven't even discussed yet such as the honeymoon location and the colors for the wedding. Jill and I look at each other after all of her questions and just laugh since we both know neither one of us has thought about any of it.

We all proceed to the table as Judy brings dinner out. She has prepared a wonderful dish of roasted duck, green beans, and smashed potatoes. For starters, Judy giggles as she places a bowl of wedding soup in front of each of us. When she settles herself at the table we eat and Judy starts an interesting conversation.

"Joel, have you had time to think of that question I asked you upstairs?"

Jill asks me what question she is talking about and I tell her.

"She asked me if I plan on using my power for good, why I am using it now for my own personal greed by throwing games."

"You know Joel, I do love you, but you are stealing by throwing these games. I was going to mention this on the way back to Indy, but it's just wrong and you know it."

"I can't even argue with you Jill. You're right, I was trying to make a comfortable life for the two of us, but I know it is wrong. Nate is the one I keep worrying about though. I brought all this greed out of him and he is slowly sliding back into that hole he was once in. If he gets into drugs again, I will feel so bad."

"Just call him and tell him it's over. He will spend some time out there before he comes back."

Judy listens to our conversation and hangs on every word spoken. I turn to Judy and say, "Is that the answer you want? I have beaten myself over the head… over and over again since you mentioned it to me. I feel so guilty for being this greedy now."

"Joel, I never once asked you to tell me your answer. The answer is inside you, and all I did was ask the question."

"You did, I should have known you would answer like a true psychologist. You answer a question with a question. I am glad you posed that subject to me because I would have tried to justify gambling for a long time."

I wake up the next day still fighting within myself, as to why I am greedy and how I could get Nate involved in something that might cause him to start doing drugs again. My conscience is not too clear right now. I have no problem with gambling if I know I will win, but when I talked to Jill before we went to sleep she told me her opinion. She thinks that I am stealing because I know the outcome of a game before it is played. Jill reminds me that Pete Rose is banned from baseball just because he bet on games that he had an advantage on. He never knew the outcome, but he had an edge. She supposes that I am further along because I don't have an edge, I know the outcome, and that makes it stealing.

After lying in bed for a few minutes and thinking about it, I realize she is right. I need to get back to Indianapolis and have Nate come back home. He needs to come back before he gets influenced by the wrong people and goes down that dark road again. I don't think I could go through another rehabilitation ordeal. Any other city and I would not mind, but Las Vegas seems to bring out the bad side in people. My thoughts races as to why I would be given this power and I can't make sense of it. I am just an average guy who has overcome a lot in his life and now I find out this strong power is mine. What am I supposed to do with it?

I get out of bed and head outside for a smoke. When I get outside, I see Judy on her swing again and she knows I have been thinking hard about my situation. She asks me if I want to talk about it and I just answer, "Not right now, I'm still trying to deal with my screwed up way of thinking."

She chuckles a bit and tells me, "Don't beat yourself up too much Joel. Whatever has been done can be fixed. You need to quit being so hard on yourself. People go through life making mistakes and never learn from them. At least you are thinking about what you've done and are making an effort to make it right. I have faith that you will make the right decision."

Maybe she is right and maybe I am being too hard on myself. I always want to do the right thing, and I really didn't need the money I won, so I didn't think about how it could affect Nate's future. If he does start doing bad things again, I will feel so awful about it. Knowing I caused someone I am acquainted with to backslide, forgiveness would be hard to give myself.

While on the porch Judy tells me of this man she mentioned to me. She tells me his name is Bill and has this uncanny knack of seeing people do evil things before it happens. He has been a recluse for years because when he gets to know people; he notices that some people are just good overall, but there are those that he can see commit adultery, steal, cheat, rape and murder. He could go to a mall walk among hundreds of people and would have endless dreams and feelings about them. Bill was so overwhelmed with this that he shut himself from the outside world and doesn't talk to anyone. I asked her if she has talked to him in person and she answers with a, "Yes." She tells me that he lives in Charlotte which is around a two hour drive from her house.

I ask Judy if we both could drive down and see him. She asks me if I am nervous about meeting him.

"Why should I be?"

I think about what she told me about Bill, and then I understand what she means. What if he thinks I will do something bad in the near future? Would he tell me everything I will do? Judy tells me that he doesn't know right away when someone will do something. She says he meets someone, or just gets close to them and that night will have a dream about them and then it comes true.

He told her that his phenomenon may sometimes take a couple weeks before he can visualize a person doing something bad. His ordeal is seeing someone he doesn't know and not being able to find them to tell them what he sees, so they can correct the future before it happens. This is what has kept him in his house for years. He blames himself because he can't find people that he has had dreams or feelings about, and he ends up seeing the bad things that happen on the news, or in the paper.

I ask Judy what my chances are that he would meet with me. She says it might depend how he feels. She excuses herself and walks back inside the house to call him. While sitting on one of the steps leading from the walkway to her porch, I take another puff from my cigarette and hear the screen door behind me open and close, Jill walks out and sits behind me with her legs straddled to my sides. I know the question is coming…

"Are you mad at me?"

I knew it, and I answer her with a, "No" as I flick my cigarette butt into the street.

We both talk for a while about what she said last night and I told her how I just laid in bed this morning thinking about how I could be so careless about putting Nate in harms way. She tells me that if he does do drugs again that it would not be my fault, because Nate is a big boy and can make decisions for himself. I tell her that I would feel so guilty if something were to happen. Jill reassures me that nothing has happened and that I should let it go.

When she mentioned that, I did let it go. It was not something to worry about, because nothing has happened. After our little conversation, Judy comes back outside and asks me how I feel about making a little road trip today to Charlotte. I agree immediately and ask her what Bill said. She tells me that he feels for someone that has a power of equal similarity and if it helps, he would be willing to talk to me.

I ask Judy what time he wants us there and she tells me that we could go later in the day and he would cook dinner for all three of us. Judy looks at Jill and apologizes for not even asking her if she wanted to go. Jill says it doesn't bother her and that she wouldn't mind being left at the house all afternoon and night by herself. Judy asks if we could talk privately up in her office and I agree.

Judy asks me to lie down on the sofa in her office, and to relax. I didn't think Jill or Judy could sense that I was a nervous wreck, but I do as I am asked and lie down on the sofa and listen to her words of wisdom. Her comments range from almost complimentary to questions that have me thinking again. She indicates that it seems to her that I may have thoughts of revenge on my mind.

My answers are short and to the point. I tell her about how bitter I am at Senator Bowman for killing my parents and how mad I am at David Johns for doing what he did to Jill. She can feel the pent up rage I have fill the room and how I want to use this power to annihilate them. I go on about how I am sick and tired of people like them getting away with hurting and using other people to get what they want.

She asks me if I have ever known someone that is a mechanic. I chuckle at first and then lift my head off the sofa and look back at her wondering where this is leading. When I answer, "Yes" she asks me if I ever had that friend fix my car. I answer, "Yes" again and then ask her where she is going with this. She asks me to think about it for a moment.

"Joel, we all use others to get what we want and need. People use friends to get what they want sometimes. While some use their ability to throw a game and make money, there are others who may use a person to climb up the social ladder. It's all about the ability to get people to do what they want, but some don't know when to stop and that's where they get into trouble."

"What does that mean, Judy?"

"You just told me that you used a friend that was a mechanic to fix your car. It's the same type of thing. People using others to get what they want. How do you think politicians and lawyers have so many friends? They know how to read people and use it to their advantage. I just have one question for you in regards to this, "Would you do the same thing if you could read people like they do?"

After thinking about it for a minute, I tell her, "No". I tell her that I know what it is like to be used by people and how it feels. I also tell I could not do something to someone that I would not want done to myself. Judy tells me that if she asked Bowman and Johns what they thought of me throwing games and they had vengeful answers, would that surprise me? My answer to Judy is that I don't think I was hurting anybody in the process. I might hurt Nate down the line, but as for now I haven't hurt anyone with what I have been doing. After talking to Judy a few minutes more we take a break, and get ready to head to Bill's house.

Jill decides to stay at Judy's home, so Judy and I head over to Bill's place.

"We barely know you Judy, and you'll let Jill stay here by herself?"

"Joel, I have people like you come to my house all the time. I keep anything of value away from here. Everything in the house isn't worth a hill of beans. I think I'll be alright leaving Jill here."

Judy smiles at me as we get in the car and go to Bill's. We arrive at Bill's in the afternoon. His place is small and quaint, but well kept. It looks as though he has channeled all his energy into this little home. As we arrive at the door he answers. Bill looked nothing as I expected. He is in his mid-thirties and is a very well groomed and clean cut man.

Once in his house, he invites us to sit in his family room, which is spotless. When Judy and I sit down he offers us a drink and we both take him up on his offer. Bill walks back into the adjoining kitchen and, as he pours the iced tea into glasses, he asks me what I am hoping to get out of this little meeting with him. I tell him that I am dealing with problems in the moral aspect of my power.

When he brings the iced tea, he looks at me and tells me that he knows what I am going to do already. He says it is rare that somebody's future comes to him so quickly, but he does point out that it does happen on occasion. Bill looks at me and asks me if I want to know what my future holds.

I think about it for a moment and answer with a nervous, "Yes". He proceeds to tell me up front that three lives will meet with a tragic ending at my hand. Bill goes further in telling me that one person is very, very close to me. After a nervous chuckle, I tell him that I would like to know more. He asks me if I want to know what my fate holds and after answering, he thinks for a moment and tells me that he refuses to respond because I may not like his answer.

My thoughts are scattered and I wonder how three people I know could have tragedy happen at my will. Bill sees my contemplation and lets me know that the future can be changed. He proceeds further in letting me know that he predicted a friend of his would die in a car accident. Bill knew what time of night and what day it would happen. His friend ended up not driving that night and his life was spared. His insight is quite revealing, but he ends his words by telling me that my fate lies in my own mind and spirit.

Judy insists that Bill stop with his revelations, so I can think for a few moments and ponder the revelation that Bill has just given me. With much thought I come to realize he is right. My future is controlled by me, my actions, my words and my control. We talk some more and then Bill excuses himself to smoke on his back patio. Judy and I talk for a moment while he ventured to the back of the house. She asks me what I am thinking and I tell her that I can not believe Bill would make such an assumption about my future when he doesn't even know me.

"It's a gift Joel, just like the one you have. He is what you need right now, so you can think about what you will do with this power you have. His insight is impeccable and for you to think that what he has said is all in jest makes you foolish."

"I don't think he is kidding, but I can't see myself hurting anyone with this power. I seriously don't think I could hurt anyone, let alone three people."

"It's like he said though, the future can be changed, but you have to make it happen. You can control it, but you have to make the effort."

Bill comes back to the room and apologizes for making me so uneasy. I tell him that it is OK because I did ask him to tell me. When he sits down I ask him what other thing will happen to me. He thinks for a moment and tells me, "You will not live to see the end of this year Joel, I am sorry."

"Can that be changed? You have me scared now! Tell me please."

"Joel, you can change the outcome, but you have to make an effort of immense proportions."

"What do I need to do?"

"You need to forget about this power you have and never use it at all."

We talk a little more and Judy sees the color leave my face as she asks him what else I need to resolve this issue. When he tells me to stay with him for two months, I firmly object. I tell him that I have a new fiancé and a life to keep in Indianapolis. But my answer is not solid and he tells me that if I do not move down to North Carolina that the temptations I deal with will be overwhelming to the point where I do not consider what is right and wrong. He says that the temptation will be too great and I end up doing what I want instead of what I should.

I ask Bill if I can go to the back and smoke. He agrees and walks me to the back of the house, and escorts me to a back deck that is just a wonderful spot to look out over his huge backyard. When I yank a cigarette out and light it, he asks to bum one and does the same. We start puffing away and he then tells me that his prediction has not happened yet, and that I should not worry too much about it, since I can change it.

We talk some more and he hits me with some ideas that overwhelm me.

"Joel, in life, it is so hard to be good. It takes a tremendous amount of effort to do the right things in life. Who gets ridiculed in life? The ones that are bad? No, it's the ones that stick to what they believe in and don't falter. *Why be good when it's so easy to be bad?*"

His words hit me like a truck. My opinion of him has gone from not liking him before I know him, to thinking that Bill is just like me. He seems to have dealt with this struggle the same way I have. I want to do the right thing, but I know, for me, it would be so easy to do wrong. Just look at what I have done with throwing those games. It was easy and I did not think it would hurt anyone and here I am acknowledging now that it was wrong, but only after Judy and Jill point it out.

As we head back to the family room, Bill pulls me aside and asks me to call him if I ever feel as though I might slip and do something stupid. He writes his phone number on a post-it and hands it to me. I do the same and tell him to me a buzz if he feels any need whatsoever to call and talk to me. When we reach the room Judy is thumbing through a *People* magazine that Bill had on the coffee table. She gets up and tells me that we should get back before Jill starts to worry. While I wait in the car, I see Judy and Bill share a few words before she leaves him. She hops in and starts the car as we both say our good-byes to Bill.

Our trip home was extremely long and very quiet. I know Judy is doing this on purpose to make me reflect on what was said back at Bill's, but I can't help thinking about how and why I will die. It is bad enough to be told that three people in your life will face tragedy, but to be told you will not see the end of the year is too overwhelming. Then I start wondering about the three lives that will face tragedy.

Bill never said they would die, he said they would face tragedy. He could have meant that with my death it could be tragic for them, but I doubted it. With everything that was said, I sure hope he didn't mean Jill would be part of this tragedy. I would die myself than to have anything bad happen to her. Then I think of Nate, Ashley and others who might be part of this list.

When we arrive home, Judy parks in the driveway and turns off the car. As I start to get out of the car, she asks me to stay inside for a minute, so that she can talk to me. She tells me that Bill likes me and sees a little of himself in me. He told her that one never thinks about having a power like this until it is thrown on them. Then to rationalize it by thinking of what good it could do makes no sense whatsoever, because it seems there is nothing good about having a power like this. He said to just let the power go and when the time is right, use it.

As we walk through the screen door, we both see Jill sprawled out on the couch with the TV on and the remote in her hand again. Judy reaches down and takes the remote and turns off the TV, and as she turns it off, Jill wakes up. She looks right at me when she wakes and smiles as she stretches. Judy asks her if she rested long enough and Jill nods.

I tell Judy that we are heading back home tonight and she tells me that Jill and I are welcome back anytime. When we head back to the room and start packing Jill sees that I am not myself and asks me what happened at Bill's. I told her what he said and Jill becomes very upset. She asked me if I believe him and I said, "No." I did tell her that Bill said that I can change the future, but that I would be tempted to use my power and the temptation may be to great to resist.

My packing is now done and Jill is still putting away her curling iron and makeup. As she packs her belongings I just lie on the bed next to her suitcase and tell her that she should not take what Bill said to heart. I tell her I know that what I do in the future will be OK and to not worry. Bill did say that the future can be changed if I do make a conscious effort.

Jill stares at me for a moment and shakes her head thinking that I am losing my mind. When I ask her what that look was for, she rips into me by saying that if I know what I am doing, why am I still betting on games when I know it is wrong. She proceeds to tell me that this self-righteous act I am pulling is just a way for me to justify it. Her words cut deep, but like always I know she is right.

I finally break down and tell her that I can't do this on my own and that I need her help. My breaking point has come, and I tell her that I have tried to deal with this alone because I know she has her problems with David. Jill looks at me and asks me what I need from her and I think for a moment and just tell her that I need her to just listen to me when I feel this awful.

My mind can't keep up with all of the rationalizing and justifying. I need her to just hear my thoughts. I know that I need her now more than ever. When she zips up the suitcase she plops down next to me and just looks at me and she sees the torture I am creating within myself. Her soft hand caresses my face and she tells me she loves me and kisses my lips gently. Jill tells me that whatever problems I have, we can work through them together.

We walk out of the bedroom and see Judy cooking something in the kitchen. When she spots us, she demands that we stay and have one last dinner with her. After we agree to stay, she tells us to set the table and that what she is cooking will not need any help from us. She tells us to relax in the family room and watch TV.

Jill and I both sit on the sofa after setting the table and then Jill slides onto my lap and puts her head on my shoulder. I tell her I am so sorry that I have these thoughts in my head and I can not make sense of them. With her understanding charm she tells me that I just need to find some sort of median and stick with it. I can't abuse this power by using it for my own greed and then try to do something tremendously good with it.

While her warm body is close to mine I just enjoy the moment with her and think about how great a future I have in store with this wonderful woman. After a few moments Judy tells us to come to the table. When we sit down we see that she has fixed yet another great Southern dish. Jill and I don't complain one bit, and as soon as the food gets passed around, Judy starts with her questioning again.

She starts by asking us if she will be invited to the wedding. We both laugh when asked and I tell her, "Of course, why wouldn't we?" Judy then pulls two gifts from behind her and places it on the table. I am shocked that she would do this and tell her it was not necessary. She tells us that the one is for the both of us. It is an engagement present, and she tells me the other is for me and for my journey with this new ability I have.

Jill opens our gift and the box under all that wrapping paper has Tiffany inscribed on the box. When she opens the box, we see two crystal champagne glasses. It was a very thoughtful gift and we both thank Judy for her warm gesture. She tells me to open mine, and as I open it I see that it is one of her books which I didn't recognize. Judy tells me that it is her new book which hasn't reached the stores yet. As I open the cover I read the note she left me on one of the inner pages.

Joel, This book is to help you through your journey of ups and downs and to keep you the inner battle within yourself from turning into a war.

Best of luck my dear friend, Judy Barksdale

I thank Judy for her thoughtfulness and ask her what the book is about. She tells me that there are chapters in it where she touches on people throughout history that have had extraordinary powers such as mine. Judy tells me that the kind of power I have has not been documented that much because it is so rare, and that no one usually makes it public because they feel embarrassed and don't want to be seen as outcasts. As I flip through the book, I see a few chapters already that already catch my interest.

We finish dinner and help Judy clean the table. When the kitchen is cleaned up and the car is loaded with our suitcases, we say goodbye to Judy and start our travel back to Indiana.

Our drive home is long and tiresome. I should have slept for a few hours before hitting the road, but I wanted to get back to Indiana to think about what I learned and felt. Jill slept the entire trip and we are now at the Ohio- West Virginia border and she still has not stirred. My feeling has been that she would berate me for being such a fool over the last couple of weeks, but she seems intent on sleeping, which is fine by me.

When we reach I-70 she starts to wake up and when she gathers herself she asks me which state we are in. I tell her Ohio and she replies with, "Almost home." She asks me if she could drive when she looks at me and notices that I am exhausted. When I tell her we will pull over at the next gas station she nods. Jill starts to smile, she loves driving my car, but with her iron foot behind the wheel, I get nervous. I don't let her drive my American beast that much, but when I do let her, she enjoys every moment.

Once we pull into the station, I fill up the tank and Jill goes inside to grab a cup of coffee. I look at the time and see that it is three in the morning. When we get back in and she starts driving, I plop my head on the pillow she brought and almost fall asleep when she asks me what I thought about our excursion to North Carolina. I pry my eyes open, but don't feel like talking. I just tell her, "It was a wonderful trip, honey, we got engaged, remember?" I try to close my eyes and get some sleep, but she waits a minute and asks me more questions.

"What kind of things did Bill say, Joel?"

"I'll tell you when I get a couple hours of sleep. I'm incoherent right now and just need a few hours of sleep."

"OK, Baby, get some rest."

When I wake up, I see that we are definitely in Indiana and I ask her how fast she was going. She said she has been coasting around 80mph, but had a little bit of a jam when we hit Columbus due to construction on the freeway. After some superficial talk she hits me with some hardball questions.

"When do you plan on telling Nate it's time to quit the betting?"

"I don't know yet."

"Do you think Judy believes what Bill said to you?"

"Yes, but I think she believes that I can change my future just like Bill told me."

"Are you happy?"

"What kind of question is that? I am always happy with myself, it's other people that get on my nerves! Quit being silly, Jill."

"I was just curious, because with everything that's happened, I can't seem to tell."

When I hear that, I just roll my eyes, recline the seat back and bury my head into the pillow again. My mind hurts with all these questions, but I know it's the coffee and she is bored senseless. She tells me that she talked to Ashley when Judy and I were at Bill's and says that Ashley is making a trip to see Nate. Her flight leaves Thursday and she wants to surprise him.

I keep hearing her talk, but my listening skills have diminished to nothing. After every few sentences she asks, "Are you listening to me?"

"Uh-huh." I keep trying to sleep, but Jill keeps talking. I ignore almost everything until Jill tells me that her parents want us to come over tonight and have dinner with them. When I sit up straight out of my semi-fetal position in the chair I answer with a quick, "No." No way am I going there after a long trip like this.

Jill keeps trying to convince me that it will be fun and that all her family will be there wanting to see the ring. I just make a deal with her, so I can sleep.

"I'll go if you just let me sleep from here to my apartment, and you have to promise me you will not say a word."

She agrees and she keeps driving and does not say a thing. Jill taps me on the shoulder and says we are home. I look up and see my apartment, smile, and then I realize I have to go to her parents tonight. Lucky me! When I unload my suitcase and take it inside I see about ten yellow envelopes on my counter. Jill had asked Ashley to bring in our mail in from both places, which she has done before in the past when Jill and I have gone on trips. As I open the envelopes, I see thousands of dollars in one hundred dollar bills in each envelope.

Jill has already gone to take a nap and I just sit, counting all the cash from these envelopes and come up with a total of one hundred fifty thousand dollars. Nate did keep his word, and I really do hope he is doing alright. I head for a nap myself knowing that tonight will be a rough experience with Jill's family.

When Jill and I arrive at her parent's house, I notice all the cars on the street and wonder how many people could possibly be in the house tonight. Jill and I walk through the door as we hear about twenty people yell, "Congratulations!" When the blood that had rushed into my head returns to my chest, I say my hellos to her sisters, mom and dad. After talking to her family for a few minutes, I try to find the nearest empty sofa, to have some alone time and recover from this madness.

As soon as I sit down, Jill's dad asks us all for our attention.

"I just want to say from the whole family, that we wish the both of you a wonderful life together."

I don't look at anyone in the room but Jill. It is a moment like this when I know she is the one for me. Her smile, long blonde hair and confident demeanor just radiate a sense of stability. She seems so happy in being with me, but I know I am the happier one of the two of us. I could never love anyone else the way I love her.

My thoughts are interrupted when Jill's sister Rachel comes up and starts talking to me. She asks more questions than Jill even does. I keep being asked, over and over when the wedding is and where we are going on the honeymoon. My mind starts spinning when Jill's dad catches me and pulls me aside to talk to me for a moment. We head out to the back deck where no one else is around. I enjoy the moment of silence until he asks the one question that I have been dreading all night.

"Have you and Jill talked about having kids soon?"

Just that thought of having children made me want to vomit, but I knew I had to keep it under control. My first reaction was to scream, but I just answer with:

"Not yet, but I'm sure we will discuss it more once the wedding and honeymoon are over."

He nods as if my answer is fair enough. We keep talking and

I bring up the Reds and ask him how he feels about picking up Jackson. Jill's dad (Frank) tells me that with the pick-up, they might just have a chance to win the division. Frank asks me if he thinks Jill and I would be interested in traveling down to Cincinnati to watch a game this summer. After telling him how much I would love to see the new ball park, Jill walks out and asks if she was interrupting anything. Her dad kisses her cheek, says, "No, sweetheart", and walks back inside, leaving us on the deck with no one around.

I tell her about the Reds game and the kid question. She gets upset that her dad would ask such a thing tonight. When I remind her that he probably knows he doesn't have much time left with his heart condition and that asking that question may not have been an unusual thing, given the circumstances. He probably wishes us to start our own family before he goes. Jill nods in agreement and starts to tear up a little. She looks over and smiles while wiping the tears from her cheeks.

When I tell her that her sister Rachel asks way more questions than she ever does, she starts to chuckle. Jill tells me that everyone in the house asked her the same questions that they were asking me. She just had to come to the deck to get away for a moment. I just look at Jill, ask her if she is ready to go back, and we head back into the house of questions.

It is Wednesday and I need to call Nate and tell him that all of this is over. Jill just left for work and I have all this time to myself, and I don't know where to start. I keep thinking about Nate being very upset and wanting me to bet some more, but I know I have to stick to what I know is best for all of us. After minutes of my internal debate, I pick up the phone and call him. He answers and I can tell he has been partying since the night before.

I tell him that we should stop betting and he rips into me saying that he just got out there a little over a week ago, and hasn't even started making serious money. When I tell him that we need to quit because we aren't doing the right thing he just lets me have it. He tells me that he has had to spend money to get things rolling. He would like to come home with a nice bank roll, but I tell him that it has to be over.

Nate calms down a bit and tells me that he wants to bet everything on one more game tonight. I know I should not bet anymore, but I do feel a little uneasy that I sprung this on him to quickly. It doesn't seem fair to Nate. After talking, I agree to bet on one more game tonight and then that is the end. He agreed that he would not bother me anymore about betting if we do just one more bet.

"Your money has increased big time, Joel. When you win tonight, you will have over six hundred thousand and I will have around three hundred."

"I would love to keep doing this Nate, but tonight has to be it. Jill pointed out to me that it is stealing, which I should have known, but I guess I got so caught up into it that I just didn't think of it like that."

I am pleasantly surprised that Nate agreed, but I could tell he was still upset about it. He tells me that he wants to stay out there for a couple more weeks and he asked how Ashley was doing. I told him she was fine as far as I knew. I did let him know that Ashley was coming out to surprise him. He tells me that she was talking to him about coming out, but didn't know if she would be able to get off work.

Nate and I keep talking for another fifteen minutes about how he should handle his budding relationship with Ashley when the doorbell rings. I tell Nate to hang on a minute, and answer the door. It's a Federal Express guy with a thick envelope for me. After signing for it, I close the door and ask Nate if he sent an envelope through Fed Ex. He starts to laugh, when I open the envelope I see a couple of huge stacks of one hundred dollar bills and ask him how much is in it.

"I sent you fifty thousand in that envelope."

He asks me how many yellow envelopes I received and I tell him the count. Nate says one more is on the way. I keep thinking how easy this is and that no one is getting hurt doing it. He tells me that he made some safe bets with our money while I was in

North Carolina and we hit big. We talk for a little while more and tell him that I will be at the game tonight.

After hanging up with Nate, I hop in the shower and then lounge around watching TV and reading the paper. I keep seeing more articles on Bowman and keep thinking about my parent's accident. When I stop reading, it hits me that I never read any articles in the paper about the accident when it happened. I was too traumatized by the end result to where I could not even bring myself to read a newspaper, or watch the news without fear of the accident being shown on TV. Memories keep coming back and I decide another trip to the library is in order to do some investigating of the accident.

I make a jaunt down to the library and park at the meter. When I walk in through the door, I see Ashley at the check out counter and start talking to her. She tells me to grab a table because she needs to talk to me for a minute. When I grab a table, she checks out a few books and comes over to tell me that her flight is booked for Vegas. She tells me that she has never been and I tell her to take some money with her, because it will be hard going out there and not betting.

Ashley keeps telling me how madly 'in like' she is with Nate. Her constant swooning about him makes me feel as though I am back in high school again. She thanks me for introducing her, but tells me that she might not be able to keep her visit a surprise because she needs to find out where he is staying. When she asks me to find out from him where he is going to be, I tell her I will find out and let her know. I tell her to swing by Jill's' after the Pacer game and I will fill her in then on what I find out.

When my conversation with Ashley is over I return to looking for information on Senator Bowman. I come across several newspaper articles about him. After reading about the disappearance of a female assistant that worked for him, it peaked my interest even more to find more dirt on him.

That incredibly hot evening in August, ten years ago, will live with me forever and this article brings it flooding back. It details my parents wreck. It was all spread out on the front page of the paper, printed the day after the accident happened. The article headlines read, *"Governor Bowman involved in deadly crash, two dead"*. I read through the article and find out that he was never tested for drunk driving at the scene. When I keep reading, those at the scene stated that Bowman didn't look as if he had been driving drunk.

My mouth starts to quiver the more I read about the same witnesses stating that my parents were the ones that looked as though they were drunk. All this time, I thought that Bowman was driving left of center and now it appears he did, but to avoid an accident. I feel so bad that all this time I went by what people told me and did not read into the facts. Senator Bowman has always been one to drink heavily, but was never caught doing anything wrong. It has been a running joke that has followed him for years. Although I believe the media does print articles that are slanted, I feel that with what I have read, Bowman had not been drinking that night.

I keep thinking to myself, what would have caused my parents to go left of center? My parents were not drinkers and I don't think that they had car problems that I was aware. Could it have been a deer? These kinds of questions keep popping into my head, but the more I thought about it, the more I realize that it has been over ten years and it is time to let it go now because I will never know the answers. Whatever I do find out will not bring my parents back and I know this is the reality, but it has been so hard to let the two people go that I love so much, and let it be a memory.

As I was reading the article I saw another one at the bottom of the page. It is about the missing assistant, and it goes on about how she was twenty one years old and had been working for Bowman for six months at the time she disappeared. I keep reading into this story. I wonder how her parents feel and if they ever found her. It has caught my attention so much that I started looking into it a little bit more.

I find numerous articles and look through them, hoping I will find out if she was ever found. My intrigue keeps mounting as I find article after article about her family and their extensive search for her. It peaks my interest so much I yearn to find out her full name and the address of her parents. Her name was very striking, Sarah Munchak. I write all this information down in an attempt to locate her mom and dad. I also notice that a Detective

Cox was not only working on this case, but he was also the detective assigned to my parents' accident. When I think about the subjects, I know I can't just go find her parents and ask about her. Maybe I should find this Detective Cox first.

I am sure that I will find more information about her through other articles, her acquaintances and at that time, a visit to her parents might be warranted. Now I need to just keep my research going and examine everything I find out about her. My own personal experience with Bowman and my parents are put to rest, but a missing intern that just disappears is quite intriguing when delving into the next potential President's background.

When I leave the library, I grab some lunch and sit on the lawn at a park close by and watch the people around me. I did bring a few magazines, but the people downtown are an amazing mix of the wealthy, middleclass and poor. It is funny in some instances, seeing all these worlds collide together. I see a makeshift preacher standing on the distant corner talking about how Jesus can save your soul and a panhandler half a block away begging people to give him money.

Then I see an attractive woman in her mid-forties walking down the street. She catches my eye because she is so attractive, but is hard to figure out if she is wealthy, or if she just dresses the type. I keep wondering what kind of life she leads and question if she is a good person or not. My thoughts keep whirling back to my personal ordeals and comparing them to this new person I have met from a distance. I imagine how many kids she may have, or what kind of tragedies she might have in her life to deal with.

My thoughts are just flashing in my mind, but I catch myself overanalyzing again and as immediate thoughts about my distant friend arrive, I banish her from my mind. Then I think about all the juvenile things I thought about Senator Bowman and realize how stupid I was to think that he might be a bad man. I feel a new goal of trying to use my power to help find this intern might keep me more focused in how to use it. It is not much, but I feel that this project would keep me from dwelling on my anger and rage towards the entire human race.

As I finish my lunch, I look up and see the lady I had running thoughts about, sitting on a bench about fifteen feet away from me, and notice her crying. I wrap up my lunch and throw it in a canister close to the bench and as I sip from my drink, I walk up to her and ask if she is OK. "No." When I ask her what happened she told me she just lost her job and came out to gather herself before she went home. She tells me she is a single mom of three and that the father abandoned all of them, six months ago. Her only way of providing for her kids was through this job she just lost.

I keep talking to her and she thanks me for my listening ear. She starts to walk away and by the time I raise my head to ask her name, she has disappeared. It startled me because I never thought anyone could disappear that quickly. I could swear she was not even ten feet away from me when I lifted my head. Well, she is gone and it shows me even more that I can not keep judging people before I know them. It goes against everything I have created in my mind.

I get heated when people talk about rumors and innuendo, and now I find out I am just like some of these people I hold such distain for. Maybe Jill is right in saying that I should just put this power aside and use it when needed, and to use this power to help others and not just abuse it for my own self motivations. My life is messed up as it is and to rationalize this power will make me go insane. I think finding out about this assistant will help me keep in the right direction, focused in helping mankind, and maybe keep my sanity more intact.

I call Nate and tell him I am on my way to the game. He seems to be enjoying himself. There is constant noise of slot machines and bells ringing and I ask him if he placed our bet. He answers with a, "Yes", and I hurry up and get down there, so I don't miss too much. I feel kind of bad that I didn't tell Jill I was going to the game tonight. She would have wanted to come, but I know she would have been angry if she saw me do anything out of the ordinary tonight.

When I hang up with Nate, I find a parking spot and hike my way to the arena. I keep walking and then my phone rings. It is Jill wondering where I am and I tell her that since I had a ticket and nothing to do, I am going to the game. She is upset and asks me why I didn't invite her. Now I'm feeling guilty and know that I should have kept my mouth shut. I can't lie to her because she always knows. She asks me if I am betting tonight on the game.

My answer didn't sit well with her when I admitted I was.

"We'll discuss this when I get home. I'll explain later, but tonight is the last night I'll come to a game and I promise I will tear up the rest of the season tickets after the game tonight."

She pauses for a moment and tells me that I better have a good explanation for what I am doing then hangs up on me. After my spat with Jill, I realize that I am at the gate and hand the usher my ticket. I scurry into the field house and take my seat. It is the end of the first period and the Pacers are winning comfortably.

I keep sitting, watching and hoping the Pacers will win without any of my help. By the third period, the Pacers have a commanding twenty five point lead and I breathe a little easier, thinking Jill will not be as mad at me if I don't have to use my power at all tonight. The game winds down, the time expires and the Pacers win again.

My trip back to Jill's is a long one. I think about her reaction to what I did or didn't do tonight and how this could affect our future. Once I pull into the parking lot I see her and Ashley outside talking in front of the stairway that leads up to Ashley's apartment. When Jill sees me, Ashley runs up the stairs and Jill stares at me for a moment, walks into her apartment and closes the door. When I get to the door I knock, Jill answers and then starts screaming at me for going. I tell her that I had to go, but I didn't use my power at all tonight.

Jill seems to be more accepting of what I have to say then. I tell her that Nate wanted me to do it one more time for his sake. He didn't like me having him go out there and only betting a couple of games. Nate didn't make as much as I did and I felt I owed him one more game. She is intent on listening to everything, and as I took the season tickets and told her that tonight was the last night, I tear up the tickets in front of her.

She looks in shock as hundreds of dollars are shredded on the floor right before her very eyes.

"Why would you do that?"

"I'm done, Jill. I can't do this anymore. I spent the whole night hoping the Pacers didn't need my help and that I wouldn't have to use my power at all."

"You still were there to control the ending if they couldn't pull it off."

"I know and I feel awful about it. That's why it's over."

Jill forces a smile and tells me she believes me. She comes over and tells me that if she ever hears of me going to another Pacer game she will leave me. I agree and tell her that I can't do it anymore. My conscience will not let me.

26

I wake up the next morning and feel like hiding in my bed for a few more hours. My head hurts and I was up most of the night worrying about Jill and me. Hour after hour I contemplated us getting a house that we can spend our lives together. I thought about starting a business with the winnings I had received, one that would be profitable after about one year. It would be nice having a job where I did not have to work that much and where it could run under the management of someone I could trust.

When I finally get out of bed, I brush the thoughts to the side and spend the next five minutes looking for some medicine for this massive headache I have. I start the coffee while Jill is still sleeping and keep searching. I find a small bottle of Tylenol in one of the kitchen drawers. After taking a few and chasing it down with some coffee, I proceed to open the morning paper. I find more articles of Senator Bowman and his landslide in the Democratic Primaries. Bowman is the hometown boy and I understand that since he is, more and more articles are going to be printed about him.

I keep reading and just gazing at his picture I feel that there is something about him I just can not like. My disgust with politicians aside, I just feel there is something about him that is very shady. The attention I'm giving these articles diminishes as I glance at the headlines on the cover of the Sports page. *Pacers, two wins away from winning division.* When I read the article I see the writer mentions the crazy games that started this winning streak. It is then that I feel guilty, because their success started with me and everyone now thinks that it is their skill or just dumb luck.

My feelings of guilt are starting again and I try to let it go, but I can't. I hate the fact that I caused all of this to happen at the beginning, but the more I think about this, I realize what a boost this team has given the city. Pacer city is now proud of something and can hold its head high about it. I just hope they do well from here on out since I will not be at any more games to give them a hand.

I hear Jill rustling in bed, trying to get comfortable. I start to grin because I know she smells the coffee, but doesn't want to get up yet. After about five minutes, she rolls out of bed and gets her morning cup and comes to the table. Her elbow is on the table propping her head up and with eyes closed she asks me, "Would you hate me if I called in today?"

"No, not really. You feel OK?"

"Just don't feel like going in. I haven't missed a full day of work in years just to call off and play hooky."

When I tell her I don't care, she gets up, calls off, and when she gets off the phone, she takes her cup and heads to the sofa where she sprawls out and turns on the TV. Her morning dose of SportsCenter awaits her. While Jill listens to the scores from the previous day she calls me over to the sofa. I put down the paper and walk over, after lying on the sofa, she takes my arms and wraps them around her and we spend the morning snuggled up on the sofa. It's a nice siesta from the rigors we both have been going through lately.

We spent all morning relaxing and she mentions that she is hungry. After negotiating, Jill and I agree to go to a local diner in town. When we both get cleaned up, I take the paper, fold it and put it under my arm and we both head out the door. Jill decides she wants to drive and holds her hand out, awaiting me to relinquish my keys. I smirk and hand them over, and she drives us without incident to the diner.

Our conversation over lunch is a peaceful one. She tells me all of her dreams for us when we get married, how many kids she would like and what she would like for me. We keep talking and she tells me she wants to go across the street and get a magazine and that she will be right back. Jill kisses me before she walks out the door. I smile when I look through the window and see her run across the street to the drug store.

I keep reading the paper and look for some interesting things to do this upcoming weekend. My concentration is interrupted by a noise I hear from across the street. It's Jill yelling at me from in front of the drug store, but I can't make out what she is saying. She yells again and starts walking back to the diner. When she takes that first step off the curb, I notice a bus coming and I realize Jill doesn't see it. My eyes widen in horror as I see the bus getting closer.

She follows my eyes to the bus heading towards her. I know she can't get out of the way in time and at this moment I feel Jill's terror. I put myself in her place and feel as though I jump backwards as hard as I can. When I come out of my mini trance, I see people from the drugstore running out and surround her where she landed on the curb. I can't see through all the people around her. I run out of the diner and head across the street.

I fight my way through the people standing there and I look in horror at what has happened. The back of Jill's head was hanging three feet off the ground on a protruding piece of metal from a public garbage container. As the drugstore owner comes out to check her pulse, my sense of feeling leaves me as I just stand there numb to what I am seeing.

Her body is motionless and I know she is gone. It is sickening to look at her hanging there like a rag doll on the garbage can. When I see the drugstore owner come back out to put a sheet over her I know now that she is dead and I weep uncontrollably. My feelings are numb and I hear people talking about what they saw.

A few people put their hands on me to tell me they are sorry, but I don't know what or how to feel. I keep thinking that just moments ago she was alive and kissed me, little did I know it would be our last kiss. I am dreading every moment I live from this point. She was my stability and the love of my life and now she's gone, just like that.

After seeing Jill being put into the ambulance covered with a white sheet my tears come again and my disbelief is still with me. I demand to ride with her to the hospital, but am denied. The EMT tells me they are taking her to the morgue and tells me to meet them there. When I see the ambulance leave I head back to the diner to grab our things.

Everyone in the diner felt bad and the owner came by and said not to worry about it. I could see some people cry as if they couldn't believe what they saw either. My head is spinning and I just sit in the booth she and I sat in and I glance over imagining her there. I start to cry again as I picture her there smiling and loving life, just moments before.

When I get up and start to walk out the door a waitress comes to me and says, "I know you don't need to hear this right now, but she left her purse in the booth. Here you go."

She hands over her purse to me as I fight back the tears. I head to the morgue hoping to have one last look at my precious Jill. I call Ashley at work to come home. I don't tell her why. I tell her to just get home as soon as possible.

The call I have to make to Jill's parents is making me sick and I can't do it just yet. It is so overwhelming to me that she was just here this morning and now she's dead. I finally find enough courage to call Jill's parents, and her mom answers the phone and I begin to cry.

I tell her of the horrible news. Her mom starts to scream and her dad takes the phone from her and asks me what happened. When I tell him, he starts to weep. I ask them both to please come to the hospital, because I need both of them more than ever. He tells me they will be there shortly. The rest of my drive to the morgue is very long and emotional.

After we arrive at the morgue, positively identify Jill and shed a few tears, her parents tell me they will swing by her apartment in a few hours. When I arrive at Jill's apartment and get settled somewhat, I hear banging on the front door. When I answer, Ashley looks at me and asks, "What happened?"

I just open my arms and hug Ashley as I tell her the news. She is hysterical when I tell her and I start sobbing again. Her emotional outburst is what I expected and I do my best to calm her. I tell Ashley to please stay with me for a few hours because I just can't be alone right now. She agrees and asks me to tell her details of what happened. I tell her that one of these days I will be able to, but for now I don't want to relive the darkest moment of my life.

After a couple hours of Ashley and me comforting each other, we both hear a knock on the door. I started to feel bad again knowing that I can't face Jill's parents. Ashley answers the door and Jill's mom and dad come in. I've always called them my mom and dad after my parents perished in the car accident. When they enter, Jill's mom comes over and hugs me. Her dad slowly walks up behind her and asks to see me in the bedroom to discuss some things.

We sit on her bed and he tells me that he has made some calls to arrange the funeral already. Jill's dad did a lot of preparation for a man that just found out that he lost his daughter. Frank finishes by telling me, "Joel, you have been through a lot lately and I just wanted you to know that we will take care of all the arrangements. When you need someone to talk to about this, we will always be here for you. We have known you so long that we consider you more of a son than a future son-in-law. What did happen today? If you don't want to talk about it that's fine, but I guess the father in me just wants to know what happened to his little girl." He starts to weep.

I know deep down that he has a right to know, but it is so hard to even tell him. My life has been crushed, but I know that I have to tell him. I have wanted to say what I feel and I just don't want to keep it bottled in, so I tell him. He starts to tear up as I tell him of our wonderful morning and afternoon, but when I tell him the details of the accident he starts to weep.

My eyes start to well up as I tell him about the condition I found her in. He asked me if I thought she suffered and I answer him honestly that I don't think she felt a thing. It happened too fast. When I tell him all that happened he says he is sorry that I had to see such a horrendous thing to the woman I love and then hugs me.

After regaining a little bit of composure we both head back into the living room. Liz (Jill's mom) and Ashley both look at us as we come back into the room. I see both of them on the sofa with Ashley's arm around Liz consoling her. It is something that I can't even fathom. God has taken my parents away and now has taken the one true person I loved so much. My anger starts to build in defiance of what has happened and I feel like blowing up.

I keep a grip on my feelings for the moment and talk to Frank and Liz for a while. We all talk about the funeral, her apartment and clothes. All of us decide it's better to get this out into the open now rather than wait when the reality of her being gone sets in. Ashley is listening and can't believe that we are talking about her dearest friend's funeral. She starts to cry when we talk about pall bearers and who we should get to do it. I tell Frank that I can't because I am an emotional wreck right now. We agree on six friends that we know will do it, and the room quiets.

Ashley finally calms down and tells me a story about Jill. It was a story of when she first started working with Jill and by the end of the story the room was filled with laughs from everyone. It was good therapy for all of us. We share many stories of Jill and how great she was to all of us. When we run out of stories, Jill's parents decide it's time to get home. Frank tells me that he will contact Jill's sisters when they get home to see how they are handling this tragedy. When Jill's parents get up, I see them out the door.

I close the door and just look at Ashley. She seems to be doing better, but it has only been six hours since it happened and she already misses her deeply. I tell Ashley how much I miss her, how much I can smell her in this apartment and that everywhere I look in this apartment I picture her there and then she disappears.

I'm done crying and just slouch in the sofa stunned at what has happened today and can't believe any of it. I keep thinking, in the next minute, she will walk through that front door saying that she's tired from her hectic day and just needs a bath, but I know it will not happen. I just wish my nightmare would end.

Ashley offers to spend the night so I won't be alone. I tell her I will sleep on the sofa and she can have the bed. My emotions can't take sleeping in her bed the way I feel and Ashley nods with agreement. When I get done telling her, my phone rings and I look and see it's Nate.

I answer and Nate tells me he is in good spirits, he goes on and on about how he would love to live out there. He has a break from his ramblings and I tell him the bad news. Nate thought I was joking and I just hand the phone to Ashley and she talks to him for a minute. She starts to tear up and tells him what happened while I just stand at the window and look out at nothing in particular. All I feel is empty inside.

When she gets off the phone with Nate, Ashley tells me that Nate is taking the first flight back and asks me if I want to go with her to the airport to pick him up. I agree with a nod and go back to staring out the window. Ashley tells me she will just spend her vacation here in Indy, so we can help each other get through this.

She tells me she is going to bed and reassures me that we will get through this. Nate calls her mobile phone and tells her to meet him at the airport at 10am. When she tells him that I am coming along he is pleased about it. I can hear him talking to her and notice he said that I shouldn't be alone. They exchange goodbyes and she hangs up the phone.

I tell her that she should get some sleep since we have to be up so early. Actually, I just wanted her to go to bed so I could have the sofa. I am so exhausted, but I know I will lie there for hours wishing Jill would walk through that door. When Ashley scurries to the bedroom, I throw myself on the sofa and quickly fall asleep, exhausted from this horrendous day.

27

We stop by the airport awaiting Nate's arrival. Our trip here was uneventful. Neither one of us could speak. I think we both woke up this morning thinking that the nightmare would be over. It's becoming more of a reality to me, but I can tell Ashley still isn't accepting it. My pain is so overwhelming and I didn't get much sleep. My couple hours of sleep were constantly interrupted by thoughts of lying there on the sofa. Jill and me and the dreams we had that can never be a reality.

I keep thinking about all I have lost in my life, and how I never really let people get to close because of it. Ashley has spent more time with me alone this past day than the years combined that I have known her. My fear is that since she knows me, she may end up being another victim. This tragic life I lead seems to be surrounded with death and despair and I am at my breaking point.

Ashley looks at me and sees that I am a wreck and asks me if I want some coffee, or something to drink. I tell her a small cup of coffee would be nice. When she leaves me there sitting at the gate Nate will be arriving at, my phone rings. It is Bill from North Carolina and I just let it go into voicemail. I pull up my voicemail and it is his voice saying, *"Don't do it, Joel. You can change your future."* As soon as I hang up, Ashley comes back with the coffee.

"What happened, Joel?"

"It's just a friend of mine, nothing important."

When Nate arrives, Ashley greets him with a huge hug and kiss. She tells him how much she missed him. Nate goes from hugging her and looks at me and comes over with a tear in his eye and embraces me. He tells me how sorry he is and how badly he feels for me. I am sure he is taking in how terrible I look, but I know it is something I can't hide right now. It has come to a point to where I don't care how I look.

Our trip back to Jill's apartment was a little more eventful. Nate told us many stories of his trip to Vegas, and I can tell he started doing drugs again. His "coked up" mannerisms and the way he wipes his nose with his index finger is the dead give away. I am too tired and upset to confront Nate about this, so I let it go for now. There is a time and place for this, and the trip back to Jill's isn't the time.

When we arrive, Ashley and Nate both sit on the sofa and I grab some huge garbage bags and head to Jill's room. I felt I should give the lovebirds some time together. I open one of the bags and start throwing some of Jill's clothes into it. This is the time to start cleaning up. It is unbearable to do it right now because I still smell her and imagine her everywhere. My senses are so overloaded right now and I start to get dizzy.

I head to the bathroom to splash some water on my face, but I end up vomiting into the sink instead. Tears start streaming down my face as I look at myself in the mirror. I'm so pale and exhausted. My eyes are bloodshot from a lack of sleep and my hair is so greasy. It looks as though I had been on a party binge for the last forty eight hours.

Ashley peeps in to the bathroom and asks how I am. She and Nate both heard me get sick and she just asked me if I were OK.

"I'm fine."

"Joel, don't worry about her clothes. Nate and I will get to them today. Just relax and take it easy."

When I get out of Jill's master bathroom I look across the room and see pictures scattered all through the room. They were pictures of Jill with her family, me, Ashley and friends throughout her brief existence. Ashley stands behind me when I walk up and grab a few picture frames just to look. I can feel my heart tearing inside my chest and I just grab a frame that had a picture of me and her. I take it with me as I walk out of her room and head to the sofa.

Nate sat next to me and puts his hand on my shoulder. He didn't say anything, he just lets me feel the pain. The tears come again and I tell Nate, "I can't believe she's gone, Nate. I just can't make myself believe it."

"I know bud, but you'll get through it. Jill would want you to."

He was right, but the feelings of loss are too raw and new. This is hitting me even harder than losing my parents. My feelings of anger towards God start to consume me again, but I don't let it take over. I ask Nate and Ashley if they are hungry. When they both answer with a, "Yes", I suggest that we go somewhere and get something to eat. Although I don't feel like eating, I know I should at least try.

I am a mess and remember that I couldn't even hold down the coffee from earlier, but I think I needed to smell her and imagine her in that room to get it out of my system. When Jill's father was here it didn't hit me because I was more worried about what he had to tell me. Now that I've had the time to think about her, I just keep losing it. When I ask them where they wanted to eat they both tell me we should go get Chinese.

We arrive at the restaurant and they order some pepper steak and some sweet and sour pork. I look at the menu and the only thing appetizing is the won-ton soup. My stomach can't take more than that, so I order the soup and some lemon chicken for later in case I get hungry. While I sit there and watch Nate and Ashley eat, I start slurping my soup and avoid eating the dumplings in it.

But when I nibble on the dumplings I realize how much my stomach is starting to growl and start inhaling the lemon chicken. Ashley and Nate look at me as though I am in some eating contest of which they weren't aware. I keep shoving the rice and chicken down my throat as they sit there in astonishment. My eyes catch theirs and I slow down substantially.

My stomach is full and I leave half of the lemon chicken. Ashley and Nate get done and we head out and go back to Jill's. I tell them that I am calling Jill's parents and ask if I can come a bit early, so I don't have to wait around for their call. They both tell me that they will start packing away some of Jill's things. I tell them just to do her clothes because I feel her parents may want some of her other things. We get back to Jill's apartment and I call her parents and they invite me to come over as soon as I can get there.

Ashley and Nate head in and I take off to her parents. My stomach is now feeling the effects of devouring too much food at one sitting. I start to drive toward her parent's place which is about a half hour away. My heart keeps aching the closer I get, knowing that her sisters will be over the top in trying to make me feel comfortable. When I arrive, I walk up to the front door and Rachel is there to greet me with a hug. Her other sister, Sarah is there behind her, awaiting her turn.

I walk inside and Jill's mom and dad greet me and ask me how I am doing. When I tell them that I can't get over her being gone, they just tell me.

"Just keep in mind, Joel that she's in a better place."

My nod in agreement is hesitant, but I honestly believe that someone like Jill is in heaven, but before her time should have come. God must know more about my future, but right now it seems very grim to me. I can't stop thinking I will be alone the rest of my life and how He could take her away from me like this. Weren't my parents enough for Him? I let go of these thoughts before I have a battle within myself here at the house.

They invite me into the living room where everyone is gathered. Her dad says a prayer before starting the family arrangements for her. It was very touching: I could tell it was from the heart of a man who deeply loved and misses his daughter. It brought everyone to tears. After composing ourselves, I start off and tell them that Nate and Ashley are back at the apartment packing her clothes and that they are leaving pictures and other things in case anyone from the family would like them.

I ask Frank if I should handle talking to the landlord about her apartment. He tells me that he has already called and they are giving us until the end of the month to get everything out of there. She had already paid the rent for the month and has three weeks left. The landlord sympathized with Frank and waived any lease penalties.

Her showing will be tomorrow and the funeral will be Saturday. It is happening so quickly. I remember having her in my arms yesterday and now I will have to bury her in a couple days. We keep talking and sharing stories. Jill's mom knew how therapeutic it had been the other day when Ashley did it. It worked again and there were tears and laughter from everyone. I couldn't take it any more and excused myself and walked to the back porch.

I stand on the porch viewing the beautiful backyard that the Zoeller's have. When I hear the screen door behind me open, I turn quickly and Rachel appears. It is sad for me to see her, because Jill and Rachel could pass as twins. Although Rachel is younger by a couple years she has the same facial features and expressions as Jill and my mind wonders until she asks me a question.

"Joel, Jill told me about your power. Did you try to use it when you saw the bus come?"

"I did but it was too late Rachel. I keep thinking about how I could have stopped the accident, but now I guess it was just her time to go. My heart is breaking and I can't stop obsessing about it. She's just gone now and I can't do a thing to bring her back. So much for any power I may have"

"Just remember she loved you more than anything Joel. I'm sure she's looking down and wanting you to get through this."

Rachel can tell that I want to be alone and walks back inside. I take to heart what she has said, but I do think about me being the one that caused her head to slam into that metal protrusion. It hurts so much to know that I may be the cause of her death, but I know that if I didn't do it she would have been dismembered by that bus. I try not to dwell on it, but I can't stop thinking about it.

I head back inside and I ask Rachel if there is anything of Jill's that she would like to have. She just says that there was a picture of me and Jill that she loves and would like to have it if I didn't want it. It was the picture I brought out of her room earlier today. I tell her she can have it and she kisses me on the cheek and thanks me. Sarah comes up and asks me to bring her Jill's book collection. Jill was a reader and had well over one hundred books on bookshelves and in her closet. She never did get rid of any one of them that she read. When I tell Sarah that I will bring them to her she hugs me.

Frank pulls me aside to the empty dining room and invites me to stay with them so I won't have to be alone. I thank him for the gesture, but tell him that I have to try and get through this on my own. I tell him that staying here for a period of time will only make me think of Jill that much more.

It probably would be better if I stayed away, so Frank and Liz don't look at me and aren't reminded of her constantly. I head out the door and as I do, Liz invites me to come over before the showing tomorrow and ride down with the family. I agree and get in my car and drive over to Mike's Place.

When I arrive at Mike's Place, he comes from behind the bar and gives me a hug. He asks me how I am doing and I tell him that I'm not so good. His kindness was unexpected and I am grateful. Mike lost his fiancé about five years ago in a car accident and I always wondered how he got through it. I ask him and he just tells me, "I'm not a religious man by any means, Joel, but God has better plans for Jill."

His comment bothers me. I tell him that God has put me through so much, that the only thing He hasn't done is douse me with gasoline and light me with a match. He shrugs off my comment with a small laugh and says, "I don't believe that crap. I know what you are going through is painful and words won't ease the pain. I know Jill was very religious and a really good person. Someone like that is in heaven now. It's all I can say."

Mike puts a Blue Moon in front of me before I take my seat. I glance around the bar and only see three other patrons. Mike comes down and talks to me and asks me how the arrangements for her funeral are going. I tell him that they are going well, but that it will be hard on me getting through the next few days.

He starts to tell me more about his experience and sympathizes with what I am going through. Mike tells me some of the things that helped him get through it. The thing that helped him the most was finding a hobby of some kind, so that I don't think about it too much. He tells me to keep going out and doing things at night so I don't sulk at home by isolating myself.

He walks away after talking to me for a while and I start thinking that my hobby could be helping the Munchak family find Sarah. It may be painful for them, but I know that it could be healing for me. Then I think. I wonder if I would rather know that my child is dead, or hang on the hope that she is still alive. I keep thinking about what could have happened to that girl. She seemed so full of life and very smart. I can't imagine anyone who could have done something so terrible to her.

My mind starts to wonder if Bowman had anything to do with it, but it ends up being a fleeting thought since I found out he had nothing to do with my parents dying. Bowman seems to be a good man in my eyes now. I didn't like how he acted in front of that little boy's funeral, but I guess I wouldn't know how he felt without being in his shoes.

I think of Bill and the voicemail he had left me. It has captured my interest and I wanted to ignore that fateful sentence he left on my voicemail. I keep thinking that one person is gone by my hand. Two more are supposed to meet with a "tragedy", but I know in my soul I couldn't kill anyone. I am angry that I have been placed in this position of no return. I have to find a way to get out of it.

The thoughts I start having are dark and hopeless. I entertain the idea of killing David Johns for his arrogance and how relieved he must feel now that Jill has passed. Jill never did get her justice here on earth and now I feel I must do something to bring justice about. If God can take away the best people in my life, I must use my power to destroy what is bad. My anger towards God aside, I must rid this earth of those few that have made life unbearable for others.

My thoughts keep racing and I think of how God has taken the ones that I love and know were good people. If he can take the good, why can't I take the bad? I could rid this earth of what is bad and evil, but would God approve? Why should I worry about that? He took what was near and dear to me and destroyed it.

How many times have men been set free because of a technicality? How many times have we seen the victim shake in shock as a guilty man walks? I am not here to rationalize. My gift aside, I feel I have to rid the earth of bad and infuse a sense of good into this pathetic world in which we live. It's how I feel, and if God doesn't approve, so be it. Every time I have cried in pain and sorrow, He has never heard me. It is time to do what I feel is right.

I see Mike and ask him for another as I sip the last of my pint. When he comes back and places a new pint in front of my face, I delve back into my thoughts of darkness. My mind has decided it is time to choose my own fate and no one else will choose it for me. All the lessons I have been taught in being a good, upstanding human being now have to be put aside for what I feel is the right thing to do.

Evil lurks around every corner and nothing seems to stop it. Why is a technicality enough to set a man free who rapes, murders, molests, burns and destroys? It is just becoming clear that the preoccupation with evil has taken over in the world, in an incredibly sick and perverse way. Jeffrey Dahmer had trading cards made of the sick and perverted ways he dismembered victims.

This country is becoming a sick and infested place and since I found my gift, I think I should use it to rid this country of the ones that are destroying it. I keep thinking of Jill and how she would advise me to handle this. She would want justice by emptying out David's wallet, destroying his career and making sure that David's wife cleans him out, but Jill isn't here now and I will have to decide where justice is needed.

My thoughts become clearer when I realize that I want to take David Johns out. I have been trying to rationalize it, but I know I will not be satisfied till he has paid for the misery he has caused. I have not chosen my fate, fate has chosen me to do this. If I had one wish, is that no one else gets involved in this horrid affair, but me and my victim.

I start to finish off the last beer that Mike brought over and realize that I need to leave, before I start dwelling on more of my unpleasant thoughts. Mike comes back over and I settle up with him and leave.

* * *

Once I leave the bar, I head to Jill's to see how Ashley and Nate are doing. When I arrive, I knock on the door and Nate answers. I ask him how things went and as I ask the question I look through the family room and see that Nate and Ash did a great job of packing away a lot of things. I ask Nate how it went.

"It was kind of easy, actually. We just started throwing all her clothes into the bags."

"Where is Ash?"

"She told me a couple of hours ago that she was meeting a friend of hers. I was starting to get worried, so I called her, but she won't answer her phone."

"She will be OK. She does this pretty often, Nate."

He looks at me and he knows I am right. We end up talking about the betting and how he wants me to start up again. I tell him once more that I can't and that even though Jill isn't around anymore, I will not do it. My thought is that I just keep corrupting Nate and I know I can't keep doing this and watch him deteriorate further. What kind of a friend would I be? It is bad enough that I have brought him this far.

Nate asks me if I want to do anything. I just tell him that I need to sleep and sprawl out on the sofa. He tells me that he will crash on Jill's bed, and heads there. I just look up at the ceiling and hope that Ashley will get home safe. It is a good way to keep my mind off of my rage and anger. As I stare at the ceiling, my mind tires and I fall asleep quickly.

"Joel, you up yet?"

As I look up, I see Nate a foot away from my face. I rub my eyes to get a better vision, but all I can do is smell Nate's nasty breath.

"Back up, Nate! Your breath could take chrome off a bumper."

Nate chuckles and heads to the kitchen and starts pouring some freshly brewed coffee for himself. While I slowly come out of my coma he asks me what I want to do today. I think for a minute and tell him that I want to keep busy and so I don't think of Jill too much. He asks me if I want to go house shopping with him and I somewhat refuse.

"I don't really feel like doing that, but if you want we can do it for about an hour or so."

Nate looks at me and tells me what part of town he wants to look in. He lets go of the subject since he knows my mind isn't in it that much. When I get off the sofa he pours a cup of coffee for me and hands it to me when I reach the kitchen. I ask him if

Ashley ever called him and he replies with a, "No." It was easy to read Nate and I knew it was getting on his nerves quickly that she has never called him back.

I tell him not to worry about it. She will contact him later and he can work it out with her then. My thoughts race as I think of something we can do today and he mentions playing a round of golf. It is a beautiful day outside. I tell him that I haven't played this year and don't want to stink, but that we could go to the driving range to practice, and he agrees.

When we get to the range, I know that Nate is getting more and more upset with Ashley. He doesn't have to say a word, I can just read him better than anyone. We both grab a bucket and start swinging away. He is using a seven iron and I bring my nine iron. My short game stinks and I always seem to practice it all year long. After I hit my first ball, Nate finally breaks down and asks, "Do you think Ashley is Ok?"

"Why don't you just try to call her again and find out Nate? She doesn't bite!"

He starts to call as I keep swinging and he gets her voicemail. After leaving her a brief message he starts to swing away. We keep hacking and after both of us are done. We empty the buckets as we head out and decide to do lunch. We head over to the clubhouse lounge, and enjoy this relaxing afternoon.

Nate talks about betting again while we are out on the patio. I see that we are the only ones out here. I feel this is the opportune time talking to Nate about his drug use.

"Nate, I've wanted to ask you about this since you came back. How many drugs have you been doing? I'm not saying it to be callous. I just don't want you falling back into that mess again."

"To be honest Joel, it's none of your business. What I do is my business. Where do you get off?"

"Well, seeing that I won us this money and you are shoving it up your nose, I think I have a reason to be concerned."

"I appreciate your concern Joel, but like I said, it's none of your business."

I am upset with him and I get up from the table and head out the exit. He follows me out to the parking lot and asks me why I am leaving.

"I can't stick around and watch you become a slave to that white crap anymore, Nate. You don't get it, do you!? I suffered a lot when you did this the last time and I don't want to see you in that position again. How much money are you down to, Nate? Did you blow it all in Vegas?"

Nate's eyes grow bigger and his face turns tomato red and screams, "It's none of your business Joel! Let it go!"

"Nate, I hope you grow up soon. Don't call me until you get some help."

I am thankful that we drove separately. It would have been an awkward drive back if we hadn't. This is too painful for me. I love Nate like a brother and I know that I will see him later on. When I leave, I realize I am alone and don't know what to do until the showing tonight. I keep thinking about Jill and then I start to wonder about what I can do today to keep my mind off of her. After much thought, I decide to get lunch at McDonald's. When I go through the drive through and get my bag, I head back to my place. I realize I need to get some clothes washed before I head to the funeral home tonight.

I get home and see my clean apartment. Jill always did such a good job of cleaning this place. I get to my room and I gather some clothes and stick them in the washing machine. I go back to the bedroom and fall back on the bed. I look toward my alarm clock and see a picture of Jill next to it. It is my favorite picture of her. She is sitting on the beach where she wrote '*I love you*' in the sand.

I just gaze at the picture for a couple minutes and put it back.

Every time I look at that picture I always feel she is still with me. It seems kind of weird, but I think I am starting to figure out that she is in a better place. She didn't like her job and I know I caused her some problems, but knowing that she is in heaven giving my parents a hard time brings me a smile.

I put the picture next to me on the bed and I doze off. I wake rather quickly when I hear the washer go into spin cycle. I glance at the clock and see that I crashed for about an hour. Jill's picture goes back next to the clock and I start gathering some more clothes for the next load. As I start another load I hear my mobile phone ring.

"Judy! How have you been?"

"Have you set a date yet?" she says with a chuckle.

After telling Judy the bad news, I hear the emotion filling her voice. She asks me if I am alright and tell her that I am in really bad shape, but trying to find my way. We talk for a few more minutes and I tell her that the showing is in a couple of hours and I need to get ready. Judy wishes me well and I tell her that I will call her after the funeral on Saturday.

When my clothes are dry, I get dressed and go over to Jill's apartment to get the picture and books for Rachel and Sarah. After loading the trunk with all those books, I head over to Liz and Franks' house. I arrive to a somber welcome from her family. It is obvious that Jill's death has finally hit them hard. I enter the house and am greeted by Liz. She tells me that Frank's heart has been giving him problems today, but he would never miss his own daughters' funeral, no matter how badly he feels.

I see Rachel and ask how she is doing. She replies with an OK, considering the circumstances. Sarah ends up telling me the same thing when I see her. Frank comes up to me and tells me that I look better than yesterday. I tell him that I finally came to a conclusion at home this afternoon that she is in a much better place, and when I came to that epiphany, I realized I could live with it.

It will be hard for a while, but I know I can get through it. Frank is amazed at how much of a recovery I have made since yesterday. My heart wants to tell him of the revenge I plan to seek out, but I don't have the nerve to tell him. This is what I am longing for now, to see David Johns get what is coming to him. I will have no remorse whatsoever for whatever I am about to do to him.

Liz tells us all that it is time to head down to the funeral home. We travel in three separate vehicles to the funeral home and when we arrive, a multitude of people are waiting outside for us. These people are friends of the Zoeller's, but a majority of the people looks as though they are Jill's friends. I remember meeting many of them and can't believe Jill had this effect on so many lives.

Knowing that Jill will be missed by them, and to think that they would care so much to come to her showing is very comforting. When we reach the inside of the funeral home, I break away from the group and enter the room where her casket lies. My pulse races as I have one last moment with her since the accident. I get closer to the casket and notice that she looks like she is sleeping. When I reach it, I become thoughtless and speechless.

I am amazed at the makeup job. She looks so much different now than when I saw her the last time. It hurts standing there alone in her presence and even though I know she is gone I tell her a few words.

"I miss you so much already, Jill. My heart is broken, but I know you are in a better place now. I just want you to know that I will take care of the unfinished business you had here, and then I can live in some sort of peace."

When I get done I feel a hand on my shoulder and when I turn around, it is Frank. I choke up and tell him how comforting it is that I had this moment with her. He tells me that everyone will start coming in soon, but if I wanted more time with her, he would keep everyone back for a few moments. I tell him it is all right to have them come in, and that I was finished.

I am still astounded at how good she looks. My eyes catch one last glimpse of her, as I keep backpedaling toward the back of the room. Rachel stops me by having me bump into her. When I turn around she asks me how Jill looks. I tell her, "She looks good". They both walk up and pay their respects to her as I find my way to the front door to get some fresh air.

As I open the front door I raise my head and end up face to face with David Johns. My hurt turns into rage in a matter of seconds and I know he feels it.

"I'm sorry to hear about Jill. She was a great person, Joel."

Joanna (his wife) was there with him and I couldn't help myself.

"Was she a great person because she was a good worker, or because she turned down your sexual favors for so long, Dave?"

David looks as though he could put me through the glass door. I said my peace and start to walk away while Joanna's mouth is still wide open in shock. As David walks inside, Joanna follows behind me and yells for me to stop. When I turn around I apologize to Joanna for talking like this when we should be celebrating Jill's life. She bypasses my comment and digs at me for information.

I tell her a few things that happened before Jill's death and she asks me about any kind of proof. I tell her as much as I know. When I give Jill's lawyers phone number to her, she thanks me, and when the tears come down her cheek, I realize they weren't for Jill. I apologize once again as she walks away and then she turns and thanks me for telling her about the situation as she opens the side entrance door.

"Joel, it's not your fault that my husband is trying to cheat on me."

"Jill didn't want to hurt you, Joanna. She liked you too much to see you hurt."

She wipes the tears from her cheek right before entering the building. While standing outside, Sarah dashes toward me and asks me what happened. I told her about David Johns and the stupid thing I said when I saw him. When I tell Sarah to keep it quiet, Rachel comes from behind and says, "Keep what quiet?"

I tell her the story, and they both start laughing. They tell me that Liz had already told them and I ask them why they are laughing. Rachel says, "We can't believe you said that to him! Jill told us what kind of man he is, and none of us have one good thing to say about him. I know that Jill is gone, Joel, but I think with those words you said to him, you've become a permanent fixture in this family."

While we all stand there in the parking lot having a good laugh, we all hear screaming coming from within the building. We see Joanna walking briskly from the front entrance to her car. David starts to jog right behind her and glimpses over at me, and then stops. His eyes meet mine, and he gives me a deathly stare. After a few moments, he heads to the car. They both get in, and he peels out of the parking lot.

I tell the girls that I want to head back in to see if things are OK. While walking toward the front door, I see Rachel and Sarah's husbands and tell them that the girls are around the corner in the parking lot. When I ask them if everything is alright inside, they both say it was just between David and Joanna. No one else was involved. I like the fresh air right now and have a desire to stay outside till some of the people leave.

All three of us walk over to Rachel and Sarah and we share some conversation. It was nothing important. I think we all started talking about the first thing on our minds to keep us from thinking about Jill. When we have a moment, I tell Rachel and Sarah that I have some things in the car for them. We take a walk over to the car. I get in and pull out the picture that Rachel wanted.

"Before I came over tonight, I stopped by Jill's and picked this up, and Sarah, I have your books in the trunk. There are hundreds of books! I have no idea where you plan to put them!"

Rachel just stares at the picture. When I ask her if she is OK she just tells me, "She loved you so much, Joel. I wanted this picture because it reminds me of how happy you two were."

"Well, it's yours now Rachel. I was so happy with Jill, but I know I can't bring her back. Don't you think she would have loved your conversation with David Johns tonight?"

Rachel just giggles and tells me, "Of course she would have."

The crowd starts to diminish and as we load up the car with the books, all four of them tell me they are heading back to the house. I head inside and see Liz by herself in the back of the showing room. She sees me and motions for me to come over. Liz tells me that she needs to get out of here because she can't take anymore.

"I know you have heard this before Joel, but parents should never have to bury their kids. It is too painful."

I nod in agreement and remind her that Jill is in a better place. Liz looks at me and says that she agrees, but the hurt will always be there.

"I know. It will be the same for me. Not a day will go by, the rest of my life, where I won't think about her. I loved your daughter unconditionally."

Liz smiles as though she had been waiting for me to say that all night. She grabs my arm and tells me, "Thanks for listening, Joel." I see Frank up by the casket. He always tries to make people feel comfortable, but I know he's hurting deep inside. His smile looks as though it is painful, but he keeps chugging along. I think he enjoys hearing the stories about Jill and how she touched the lives of the ones that came tonight.

I tell Liz that the girls went back to the house. When I see that Liz and Frank are doing fine, I head back outside to get some air again. Funeral homes have always been terrible places for me. It sickens me that tragedy is something that brings families together. Relatives that you haven't seen in years will show up and you reminisce about days gone by. I have never figured out why that happens, but I do know that since my parents died, I haven't seen any of my relatives.

They always said if I needed something they would be there, but how can someone be there when they live in San Francisco, or any other part of the country. It just seems that the longer the distance a relative is from you, for every five hundred miles away, a year is added until you see them the next time. My parents dying makes me uneasy whenever I enter a building like this, but the sorrow from everyone that enters that front door depresses me to no end and I have to get out just to get some fresh air and be away from it for a few moments.

People keep filing in and the occasional friend of Jill's comes up to me throughout the evening, asks how I am doing and tells me some more stories of Jill, and what she meant to them. It is very refreshing to know that Jill affected so many people in a positive way. I am grateful for the time I did have with her, but I just don't understand why such a great person as Jill could be taken so quickly.

It gets late and as I say my goodbyes to Liz and Frank and

walk over to Jill's casket one more time to get a final look at her. I leave the funeral home and go back to Jill's in hope of finding Ashley. She never showed up, and Nate didn't either. Nate I can understand. Jill was never fond of Nate, but he was very respectful of her. She didn't like him after the whole drug ordeal and Nate worked very hard after that to win her approval.

I just can't figure out why Ashley wouldn't show up for her best friends showing. Ashley said she wanted us to be a support system for each other while we try to get over Jill being gone, but I never thought she would miss tonight. Then I start to worry about her not coming home last night. She may have used her vacation time to go back to Columbus, but I know for a fact she would have called me or Nate.

My call to Nate is a strange one. I call hoping he doesn't get an attitude with me, especially since I told him I didn't want to hear from him again until he got some help. He answers and I ask him if he had heard from Ashley. "Nope, I haven't heard from her at all." I try to ask him something else and he hangs up on me. I guess it's something I should have expected since I did put him on the defensive today.

As I pull into the parking lot at Jill's I see that Ashley's car is not there. My thoughts start again, but I do remember again that her funeral is tomorrow. Ashley would never miss her funeral and be able to live with herself. Since I am already here, I decide I will spend the night on the sofa. When I get inside I check Jill's answering machine and there are no messages. I stretch and then go head first onto the sofa where I fall asleep almost immediately.

I get up in the morning when my cell phone rings. It's Liz and she wants to know if I am meeting the family at the funeral home, or at the house. My sleepy eyes check the time and I see that it is almost 10:00 a.m. I tell Liz that I will have to meet them at the funeral home. When I hang up with her, I start out the door needing to get home. I have to get some new clothes on and desperately need a shower.

Arriving at my apartment, I see a note on the door. It is from Nate apologizing for his outburst yesterday and he says he wants to talk to me. I open my door and call him to see if he wants to head to the funeral with me. My conversation is short and to the point. When we agree that I will pick him up before going to the funeral, I hang up with him and get a quick shower. I get dressed and head out the door.

My arrival to Nate's apartment is quick. He hops in my car while it is still running and we head off to the funeral. It starts at 11:30 a.m. and we are pushing for time. Nate tries to talk, but

I tell him that I am not mad, but have other things on my mind right now. I tell him that we can talk after the funeral if he wants. He agrees and apologizes for not being there last night. Nate said he didn't want to come and make me uneasy with what happened with us earlier yesterday, and then seeing me so quickly afterward.

I accept his apology and when we arrive at the funeral home I ask Nate if Frank asked him to be a pall bearer. Nate states that he is somewhat of an alternate, but no one contacted him today to be one. He figured Frank filled the position. We head inside and I introduce Nate to Rachel and Sarah. Liz and Frank have known Nate for a while now and come over to us just to say hello. When introductions are made to Rachel and Sarah's husbands, we head into the room where the ceremony is about to begin.

It is a short ceremony and very religious. Pastor Stevens talks about Jill and her life here on earth and that she is in heaven now. It's the same kind of presentation that he did at my parents' funeral years ago. After he is done, he invites the pall bearers to come forward after saying a prayer. There is silence in the room for a couple of minutes. A small organ is playing background music of old hymns and we all sit in quietly, awaiting our release to the graveyard.

It hits me. I will never see Jill again. It is just unbelievable that she is gone, but I don't think I grasped it until now. I'm just glad I was able to say goodbye to her last night. The ache in my heart starts to come back and I start to cry as Pastor Stevens closes the ceremony and directs us to the gravesite.

Nate decides to ride along with me to the cemetery. He said he didn't want me thinking about her the entire way there. I did agree with him that if no one came with me I would probably think of her the whole way and be a even more of a mess. We put the flag on my car for the funeral procession and wait. The hearse finally starts to leave and all of us follow.

The trip to the gravesite takes us about half an hour and upon arrival, I can see Liz getting out of the limousine crying. She has been so strong up till now, but I think the reality has finally set in. We gather around under the tent that was set up for this occasion and her casket is brought in by the pallbearers. Pastor Stevens's message and words are touching, but this whole salvation thing makes me uneasy. It makes me uneasy because I am still holding on to my anger toward God and questioning why these kinds of things happen to the ones I love. I will deal with this issue at a later time.

When the final ceremony is over, I see everyone leave and I just sit there in my chair and look at Jill's casket right in front of me. The emotion overwhelms me, but instead of weeping, I get up and head toward my car. I see Nate waiting for me at the outside of the tent and he asks how I am doing. I tell him I am fine and then we leave. While driving I tell Nate, "The Zoeller's are having a get together at their house. You are more than welcome to join me if you want, but if you don't, I can drop you off at home."

"Just drop me off at home. I don't feel up to it and you will be occupied the rest of the day with this. No offense, but it will depress the hell out of me, Joel."

With a nod, I take Nate back to his place, drop him off, then head to the house. When I arrive, I see cars parked up and down the street and try to find a place closest to the house. I park, get out and walk toward the house. Rachel is outside the front door, waiting on me to arrive. As soon as I meet up with her, she asks, "Did you see Ashley at the funeral today, Joel?"

"No, I didn't and to be totally honest, I didn't even think about it today until you mentioned it. I was in such a rush to get here, I guess I forgot."

Rachel tells me that she is afraid for her. She tells me that Ashley talked to her the other day and said she wouldn't miss Jill's funeral for anything in the world. I can tell Rachel is nervous and I try to let her know that she may have been too upset to come, and ended up going to her mom's in Columbus to get over this. I reassure Rachel that Ashley has left like this before and always turns up again.

She breathes a sigh of relief, but I can tell she is still concerned. It is funny how I recognize Rachel's mannerisms and the faces she makes. Jill and Rachel share so many of the same mannerisms that make it easy for me to read Rachel without her saying a word. When I walk into the house, I see many strangers. I scurry through the house looking for someone I know.

I finally get tracked down by a couple of people that went to high school with Jill. They found out by word of mouth she was engaged to me. After awkward conversations with them and others, I notice people start to file out slowly. I spend the rest of the time on the back deck and try to enjoy the beautiful spring weather. It has been unseasonably warm and I heard on the radio that we have had twenty straight days without any rain, with no rain in sight for another week.

As a slow breeze comes through the backyard, I hear the screen door slam. I look up to see who it is. Frank comes over and sits in a chair next to me. He asks me what my plans are now that Jill is gone. I told him I really haven't thought about it. My life has been such a whirlwind since she died and I haven't put any thought in what to do now. I tell him that I might move away, since everything in this city reminds me of her, but I don't know yet.

Frank tells me I will always be a part of his family, and tells me that I am welcome to visit anytime. He tells me that when it is time for me to leave today, Liz has something she needs to give me. I tell him, "Alright." He gets up and heads back into the house. I keep hearing the crowd leaving. When I hear no more voices permeating through the back screen door, I head back in myself.

I get in and see that everyone has left. Rachel and her husband, Sarah and her husband, Liz and Frank are the only ones left, and all are sitting together in the family room. The room looks as though a bomb had just gone off, much to my surprise. I ask if they need any help cleaning up. Liz tells me not to worry and that she has something to give me. She waves for me to follow her as she walks out of the room.

We get to the kitchen and she tells me to wait here. She comes back and hands me a little velvet bag with a couple of drawstrings. I open it up, and as I do, she tells me that the funeral director gave her this before the funeral today. It was the engagement ring I gave Jill. Liz told me she didn't want to give it to me in front of the family. I nod and start to tear up. She gives me a hug and I tell her I have to go.

"I understand, Joel, just be careful."

I say my goodbyes to everyone, knowing that I may not see any of them in a very long time. Jill is no longer around, so why would they need me, or want me here? It would just remind them of Jill any time I came over. I leave and head to my apartment.

When I wake up Sunday morning, I drag myself out of bed and head to my lounge chair. I plop myself down and turn on the TV. I flip through about thirty channels before putting it on CNN, so I can listen to the news while I brew some coffee. As I put the filter in, I see that the Reds won again and I can't believe how much of a boost Jackson has given them. Then I think about Jill not being able to see her beloved team doing so well. I think about it as I pour the coffee grounds into the filter.

As the coffee is brewing, I head to the chair and just gaze at the TV. I don't pay attention to anything I am seeing, because I am thinking about how much I miss Jill. I force myself to stop thinking, get up and pour a cup of coffee for myself. The book Judy gave me is sitting on the kitchen counter. I had forgotten that I brought it back from Jill's yesterday. I start to read.

Judy has written so much on how people handle their dubious powers. She starts by telling how people that have these certain abilities usually are waging a battle within themselves as to how they use their power wisely. I read about some people that can foresee the future, use their power for selfish gain and end up changing their futures disastrously. Reading more deeply into the chapter, I see where she has written about those that have used their psychic powers to control life and death.

My mind begins to wonder if I have the power to control ones ability to *live*. Do I have the power to kill just by hoping I can stop a beating heart? If I do have this power then why am I not going around making people like each other, and why have I just used this power for my own personal gain?

I start to think about how much I despise David Johns and how much I want to rid the world of this disgusting excuse of a human being. Then I start to delve deeper into the situation and try to think of some sort of political justification for killing David. What would have happened if the leader that ordered the slaughter of thousands of Rwandan's had been assassinated before he took all their lives?

Would the person that assassinated him been ridiculed forever or celebrated? What if this assassin knew something beforehand that we didn't and took matters into his own hands not caring about the consequences? If I did change something that could affect the future of the human race, would I go through life with a majority of people hating me, and wishing me a slow painful existence? I still won't know the answer to that until the opportunity arises and I act upon it, if I do.

I keep thinking about those that die at the hand of a mad man, and the assassin ends up in prison, or hung in the gallows. David Johns is in no way a comparison to Hitler, but could I live with myself if I took his life? I know I could if I had taken the life of Hitler.

With this breakthrough I can live and breathe not having to

worry about using my ability wondering if God would be pleased. I have a hard enough time doing the right thing without this ability getting in the way. If I just look at every situation strictly as a good or bad situation, I can make a solid judgment. My ordeal is whether I should rid the world of someone that I know is bad. I have a power that would let me kill someone and get away with it.

My opinion of the question, '*Would God be pleased?*' goes right out the window. I have trusted in Him too much only to be hurt repeatedly. It is time I do what I think is right and not what I think He would want me do. To see my family dead and now my future wife killed, I have lost my faith in God and really don't care what consequences await me. I am feeling the anger and rage take over, my pulse races when I think of Jill being gone and David Johns still being on this earth.

I sip down the last of my coffee and pour another cup. My blood pressure is rising and my anger is at its highest level ever. While sipping my coffee, I finally feel the need to pay David a visit at work tomorrow. As soon as I think about my feelings and rage towards David, my mobile phone rings. It's Judy. She tells me that she was hoping to catch a plane to come to the funeral, but wouldn't have been here in time. I tell her it's alright and about what I have been thinking this morning. She asks me to go on, intent on helping me.

"I have a strong inclination to take out David Johns. I know it's wrong, but Jill never did get her justice when she died. My thoughts were about Rwanda this morning."

"Joel, I don't like where this is going."

"Just hear me out, and then tell me what you think. If someone could foresee the future and assassinated the leader before he ordered all those people to die. Would the assassin have been condemned by everyone around him? These are the thoughts that have made me want to kill David Johns before he hurts someone else."

"Joel, losing Jill is devastating, I know. Did David kill her? No! You need to get off of this God complex you have started for yourself and take care of things around you. Spending time dwelling on revenge, anger and rage will only make you dwell on the bad and not the good. Think about this life you have. You need to treasure your life here on earth. Life only comes around once and you should value every moment of it."

"I guess you're right, Judy. It's so hard knowing that Jill will never be here to see David get what he deserves. Knowing that David will walk away from this ordeal makes me so angry. For him to get off without a blemish on his record will stay with me until he is punished."

"I take it you ran in to him over the weekend?"

I tell her what I said to him and she starts to giggle a bit. After telling her the story I say that I kind of feel bad that I said it with his wife there, but I couldn't help myself.

"Maybe you should apologize to him."

"Why? He treated Jill like crap."

"Do it for yourself. It might be a good way to start a new way of living and thinking. Having an apologetic and forgiving spirit might be the best medicine for you, Joel."

"You're right, but it will be tough. I was planning on making a visit to him tomorrow anyway."

"There you go, Joel. You may just start becoming a better person because of it."

When I think of going to the office, it hits me again that Ashley has not been heard from. I think about calling her mom to see if she traveled to Columbus, but if she hasn't then I would hate to listen to her worry and call me every second until she showed up. I give Nate a call on his mobile phone and he doesn't answer. My guess is that he hasn't heard from Ash yet, because he more than likely would have called me if she had contacted him.

It's time to rid myself of the anger and rage for a few moments while I get cleaned up. I take a shower and get dressed hoping that my anger will subside. The only way I can find any peace in my life now, is by getting rid of David, but deep down I know it is just a feeling and acting on it would be unforgivable. There is no way I could forgive myself if I took someone's life.

I finish cleaning up and head over to Jill's apartment to get whatever clothes and belongings I have left there the past few years. It seems like such an effort going through her apartment just to get a bag full of old clothes and some pictures. While pulling up to a parking space at her complex, I see her parents decided to skip church this morning and have a look inside the apartment. When I walk in they both greet me with a smile and a warm hello.

They both tell me that they started packing up her clothes and donating a majority of things to charity. Liz tells me that she took a few things, told me what they were, so I could give her my blessing in taking them. I just nod and notice how empty this place has become. Some of her furniture is missing and asked Frank if he had any help moving it. He tells me that Rachel and Sarah's husbands came over and took what they wanted and packed it up on Frank's truck.

After talking to them for a few minutes, Liz tells me that they're coming back for a second load. I tell Frank to relax and that I would help Steve and Josh load up the truck next time. When I stroll through the bedroom, I see that it has become barren. We shared so many good times in this place. It may be without furniture, but still loaded with lasting memories. Reality sets in and I start to cry. As I wipe the tears away I hear Liz calling, asking me if I wanted anything to drink.

"The coffee I can smell would be fine."

I can tell that it's Jill's Kona brewing. What a shame that she is gone and can't enjoy the simple pleasures anymore. Maybe Judy was right. Living a good life from this point may not be a bad idea. To dwell on the bad makes me forget the things I take for granted. Listening to birds chirp first thing in the morning, and the smell of coffee brewing, when you first wake up. My list is endless when I start to think about it.

Liz hands me a cup and see that I have been crying. She smiles and reassures me that Jill is in a better place.

"You know Joel, I hate funerals too, but what I kept hearing through the entire weekend was how much Jill had affected people's lives in a positive way. I realized how lucky I was to have her as *my* daughter. She's gone, but with the way she helped so many friends and family members, her memory will live on."

"You're taking this very well, Liz."

"I just realize now that she's gone how proud I always was to be her mom. She was my angel and now I guess God needs her more than we do."

I nod slowly thinking that this God stuff is getting old. Every time I hear "God", I want to scream. The reality is that she was robbed of having a life here on earth. She will never have the opportunity to have kids, grandchildren, or be with me. Why couldn't it have been me that died? I feel so lonely now and miserable. She had a happy life ahead of her while my life is now spiraling into a bottomless pit of anger and despair.

Steve and Josh come back and I help them load the truck. While helping them, I think of how I will approach talking to David. After thinking about it for a few minutes, I decide to just apologize about my behavior at the showing and see if it helps me feel better. We get done with the second load. Steve and

Josh drive off again as I walk back into the apartment. I sit on the floor with my back up against the wall as Liz and Frank say their goodbyes to me.

I ask Frank when he expects to have this apartment ready for the landlord. He tells me he is coming back later to get rid of the small boxes lying around. Liz is going to vacuum the entire apartment and then will hand the keys over tomorrow. I tell him that I have a copy of the key that goes to the front door. He tells me not to worry about it and to just slide it under the door when I lock up.

When they leave, I just sit there and stare at the empty wall in front of me. Her entertainment center used to be there, but now is just an empty wall. I think of all the times we had here, most of them were good, but some were bad. Silence fills the room, to the point where it is almost deafening. I shake my head and realize I have to get out before my depression starts up again.

32

It's Monday and I wake up with anticipation. A stop by David's office might be a good thing to do, but I am so nervous about seeing him. I should call before I go down, but if he isn't there, I know I can make a stop to the library. After getting dressed and drinking a few cups of coffee, I hop into my car and head downtown. I park my car at a meter and my heart starts to race.

David may not even be in the office, but I know I must at least try to see him and apologize. My words Friday night were way out of line. It was a moment of an emotional outburst, but it was neither the time, nor place to do it. My heart races more with each step I get closer to the office. I see the guard at the desk and tell him that I am here to see David Johns.

He tells me to sit in the chair across the lobby, and his secretary will come down to get me. I get nervous and feel faint. My palms start getting clammy. When I look up to check the time on the clock above the guard's desk, I see a woman coming my way and she tells me that she is sorry to hear about Jill. She states that she was at the showing Friday and introduced herself.

I do remember her being there, but I can't remember her name. Jill introduced me to her a couple years ago at a company party, but I still can't remember her name. She tells me, "David, would like to see you."

"Did he seem upset when he found out it was me?"

"I don't think so. He's just very busy today, but was intrigued that you would want to see him."

"I just wanted to apologize for something I did Friday."

"I was there when it happened", she whispers. "You were so out of line, Joel, but you were so right. But don't ever repeat that."

We exit the elevator to the twelfth floor and I follow the secretary to his office. I am walking behind her down the hall. I hear his boisterous voice throughout the office, as he talks on the phone. She asks me to wait outside the office. I don't hear any more words coming from his office. A click is heard as though he is hanging up the phone.

His door opens and he glances down to where I am sitting.

"Joel, what brings you here?"

"I just wanted to apologize for the other night."

"Please, come in and sit down."

We both enter and he takes a seat in his executive style chair. He asks me to close the door behind me, so we have some privacy.

"You have a lot of guts coming here today, Joel."

"I know. I'm so sorry for my words that night."

"I am very upset with you, but there are a few things I need to tell you."

"Such as…?"

"Jill was a valuable member of this organization, but to tell you the truth Joel, her work was pathetic lately. Her little stunt of trying to file a lawsuit against me was way out of line. What I am trying to tell you is that she would have been fired within a week, if she were still alive."

"Why would you say such a thing? Jill is gone. Why even tell me that you intended to fire her? I came to apologize, but now I know you don't have a forgiving heart at all."

"I don't, Joel, remember that I am a lawyer. None of us are known for having a heart."

"If you are trying to get back at me for Friday, you are doing a good job of it."

"Joel, you pathetic excuse for a man. I want you to know that because of you, I have been kicked out of my house and my wife is threatening a divorce."

"Well, Dave, maybe if you kept your stick in your pocket this wouldn't have happened. Your wife talked to me Friday night and I gave her the number for Jill's attorney. I told her that Jill had video and audio of you making advances. If anyone in this room is pathetic, it's you, Dave. Why did you ever think you would get away with it?"

David just stares at me. He knows now that he has lost the upper hand. His demeanor changes from being offensive, to a defenseless gnat. My stare back at him is cold and my anger starts to boil again.

David starts to talk again and with a quiet voice says, "If my wife divorces me, I will come and have you taken out. You understand where I am going with this?"

"I certainly do, Dave, but first I want to show you something."

"Show me what?"

He sits back in his chair anticipating. I feel as though I am right in front of David. I take his hand and smack him right across the face.

"What the hell just happened?"

"I made you hit yourself, Dave. Now listen, you ever come after me, I will do much worse that just having you hit yourself. Do you understand where I am going with this?"

"Your idle threats are just like Ashley's. Do you know where she is, Joel?"

At this moment I realize David may have had her killed.

"No, but I have a feeling you do."

"All I can tell you, Joel is that it is pointless looking for her. She's gone."

My blood boils with rage and anger. I make David take a pen off his desk and write on a piece of paper. *I, David Johns, took the life of Ashley Johnson. I paid someone to have her killed.* He puts the pen back down on the desk. His look of horror, knowing that he can't control his physical movements, is gratifying.

I look across David's desk and I have him pick up his letter opener. He tries to speak, but I feel as though I am strangling his vocal cord. His silent scream is unheard by anyone as he cuffs the base of the letter opener in the palm of his hand and drives the tip into his throat. Blood from his severed artery is spurting on the office walls as he gasps for a tiny breath. I don't even allow him that as he bleeds to death.

I open the office door, and yell for someone to call 911. His secretary comes in and immediately screams. A few lawyers in the office come in and pull me out of the office. One asks me what happened. I tell him that David stabbed himself after writing a note that's on his desk. He tells me to sit in the same chair I sat in before entering the office. The screams of women throughout the floor are piercing my ears. I try to regain my strength which has diminished throughout this entire ordeal. When I did this to David, all the energy I used to kill him makes me feel as though years of my life were peeled away.

It is chaotic in his office. I could tell people are trying to save him, but I know for a fact he is gone. There is no way he could survive with that much blood leaving his body. One of the lawyers comes out and tells me not to move. I tell him that David killed himself.

"I had nothing to do with it! I never laid a hand on him! He did it to himself!"

He looks at me in shock. I am told to stay and not move. After waiting for ten minutes, I see David's lifeless body being wheeled out of the office on a gurney. A white sheet is draped over him, as the blood stains penetrate the sheet, so all can see the horror. When his body is wheeled away, a homicide cop comes up to me and asks me some questions.

This cop looked as though he had been to many scenes like this. He is an older gentleman, maybe in his early sixties. His face is worn and tired; he has the look of a man that has seen crimes that I only have nightmares about.

"Hi, I'm Detective Cox. Did you have anything to do with this?"

"Not at all! He killed himself."

"I don't think you did this, Mr. Warner. You are wearing a white oxford and you don't have a drop of blood on you, and if the evidence shows he did it himself... we will let you go. Wait here."

I sit and wait for almost two hours. A cop is sitting with me, so I can't leave the premises. When this investigator comes back, he says that I can go. As I leave he asks one more question.

"I don't understand why he would do this in front of you. Can you help me to understand?"

"I came here to apologize for something I said to him at my fiancées' funeral. He picked up a pen, wrote something down on a piece of paper, then took the letter opener and offs himself. It was all too bizarre to even comprehend, let alone explain."

He asks me to come downtown for questioning. I agree, asking him where I should meet him. He scribbles an address on a piece of paper. After looking at it, I ask him if I should ride there with him.

"It isn't necessary. Just meet me there in half an hour. "

I wait patiently outside the station, waiting for Detective Cox. It has almost been half an hour since I arrived. I glance toward the entrance and see Detective Cox walking up the stairs. I get out of my car and yell his name. He waits for me to catch up with him. We enter the station together and he tells me, "This may be awhile. It is customary that we do this."

"Do what?"

"Haven't you seen cop shows on television? I brought you in for questioning, Joel."

"I thought I already answered them back at the office."

"I'm still not done, Joel."

He walks me into a room with no windows. A pen and some paper are on the table while another detective sits in a chair at the table. He seems as though he is ready to pounce on me with numerous questions. Detective Cox leaves and Detective Jewell takes over.

Hours later the questions keep coming. A lot of the questions were ones that I answered back at the office, but I know what Jewell is going after. He wants me to change an answer so he can nail me on a lie. I don't change an answer that I have already given. I'm sure he notices the consistency in which I answer the questions. I am just glad he is asking questions about the actions that took place in the room. If he asked more about what went on in my mind during the suicide, I don't know if my conscience would have let me off the hook.

When he leaves the room, Detective Cox comes in and apologizes for keeping me there so long. He hands me his card asking me if there is anything else I can remember that could help him. I think for a moment and just shake my head. My mind is tired from all the grilling. He asks me one more question.

"There is one last thing. Do you know an Ashley Johnson?"

"She is my fiancées' best friend. Why?"

"It looks as though David came clean before he died. He admitted having Ashley murdered. That is what he wrote on the paper before he committed suicide."

I shake my head in disbelief as I walk toward the exit. My heart starts to get heavy with guilt. I just killed a man and will get away with it, if my conscience doesn't take over. David Johns should have kept his mouth shut, or he would still be alive. I lost Jill and to tell me Ashley is "gone." How would anyone react?

While walking towards the exit of the building, I see a crowd of reporters standing outside the station. They stand there hoping to be the first one to break any kind of story about what has happened today. I ask a cop at the desk if there is another way out of the station. He tells me that I have to exit through the front. I exit through the swinging doors and about twenty reporters swarm me like bees to a hive. I am asked many questions in regards to David Johns death. After saying, "I have no comment" over and over, I walk to my car. Reporters follow me as though I might change my mind and speak with them.

I stop in the middle of my jaunt back to the car and turn around. A few reporters ask me how David Johns died. When I tell them the details of his suicide, they all have a look of shock on their faces. They can't believe that David would commit suicide. When I tell them David wrote a note before killing himself, saying that he had Ashley murdered, they all look in disbelief.

It is a good feeling, making Indianapolis finally see the corruption, callousness and dishonesty this man exuded. He was definitely evil. When he told me about Jill, and that he was going to fire her, how he claims he had Ashley murdered, all reinforce my not feeling guilty in taking his life. I felt guilty about the way I did it, but with all that was said, with time to think about what I had done, I still feel David deserved to die.

Acting as jury, judge and executioner, is quite refreshing. Especially refreshing, when I know the guilty party is as evil as they come.

33

On my way home, my mobile phone rings and it's Nate. He is at my apartment and wants to talk. I tell him that I am on my way there and I ask him, "Is anyone from the press standing around my apartment building?"

"Not that I can see. Why?"

"I have some bad news about Ashley, Nate."

"What kind of bad news, Joel?"

"I went to see her boss today and while I was talking to him, he wrote a note and then stabbed himself with a letter opener. He bled to death right in front of me. In the note he stated that he had Ashley murdered."

"I can't believe this. What reason would he have to kill Ashley?"

"Don't know, Nate. All I can figure is she knew too much about the lawsuit that Jill was going to bring down on him, so he killed her. She can't talk if she's dead."

"Joel, I think I am going to be sick. I heard on the news today that David Johns killed himself. It is the same guy, isn't it? You didn't do anything to take him out, did you? With your power and all, you wouldn't use it to kill anyone, would you?"

"What kind of stupid question is that?"

"Just thought I should ask, Joel."

"I will be there in a few minutes."

I hang up the phone and I realize that I am lying to my best friend, Nate. It bothers me to be a murderer, but not to lie about it. I don't know how much more I can lie and deceive the people around me. Look at what's happened. My intentions were good. I just can't admit to anyone what I've done, or I could be charged with murder. The police may not believe my story, but I can't take the chance on this getting out of hand.

When I arrive to my place, I am shocked that no one from the press is hounding my apartment. I open the front door and see notes on the floor where people slid them under the door requesting interviews. As I close the door, I see Nate follow right behind me. I invite him in. As he walks through the front door, I see that he looks thinner in his face. It's almost as if he is a skeleton with skin.

I ascertain from his mannerisms and personality change, it could be only one thing, heroin. While talking to Nate, he brings up the betting again and I refuse. He tells me he needs money badly. I ask him what he has done with the thousands of dollars he won.

"I spent it all, Joel. I didn't think you would quit betting, so I partied and spent tons of money on women, booze and drugs. I admit that I do have a problem, but I intend to get help."

"Okay Nate, I will pay for rehab again, but I refuse to bet anymore. I feel badly that this betting, which I thought was harmless, has destroyed your sober state and turned you back into the man I remember, before you went to rehab the first time. I will not give you money anymore, Nate. I can't give you money knowing that it's possibly going toward a needle, or some powder."

"C'mon, Joel! I'm begging you, please!"

"I can't do it anymore, Nate."

"Then just forget it, Joel."

Nate grabs his things and takes off out the front door. I can tell he owes big money to somebody, just by the way he is acting. I would have helped him if he would come clean about how much he owes, but I can't pay for something he will not tell me about. Nate is about to hit rock bottom, but giving him money, will just go into the habit he has come to embrace again.

My senses reel as I turn on the television and listen to the top story. It is about David. A reporter is standing outside David's office building. There I am on the television. I didn't think I looked that awful! It's about my wonderful account of what happened today. It shows me talking in detail about David and what he did in front of me. I get sick of seeing myself and reliving the moments of the day, so I turn off the television and try to think of something else that could keep me occupied.

I think of the assistant that disappeared and wonder if today is a good day to start looking for her. While reading some of the papers I brought home from the library, my eyes focus on a section about the detective that was on the scene of my parent's car accident. Detective Cox told everyone at the scene, that the wreck was an accident. How would he know already if it were an accident? After reading about him more, I realize Detective Cox is the one I saw today. I'm sure it is the same one.

My phone rings and it is Bill again.

"Don't kill anymore, Joel."

Before I could answer, he hangs up. I try to call him back, but he doesn't answer. I will call Judy and ask her if she can help me handle this tremendous guilt I have. My fingers tremble as I dial her phone number. I disconnect before the call connects, so I don't have to hear her tell me how wrong I am. Honestly, I don't care what she has to say. I know she would have killed David if she had the same power that I possess. If the same words were uttered from David, I know, for a fact, she would have wanted some sort of justice right then and there.

I throw myself on the sofa and I hear someone knocking on my door. When I answer the door, I see that it is Detective Cox. I invite him in and he asks me a few more questions. As the detective sits in my wingback chair, he asks me, "Mr. Warner, some things aren't adding up. I just don't understand how David Johns would do something like this. His wife kicked him out of the house, he knew he was guilty of having Ashley murdered, but he just wasn't the kind of person to do something like this."

"I know, Detective. I am still in shock over it."

I ask the detective if he has a name. He answers, "Larry Cox."

My eyes widen as he looks on the sofa and sees copies of newspaper articles that I threw on the floor about Sarah Munchak and my parents' accident. He glares at me with a gazing haze, he then asks me, "What is this, Mr. Warner?"

"You can call me Joel, Detective Cox. My parents died in a car accident years ago and my curiosity caused me to investigate further how they died. I know for a fact neither one drank, so it just seems the whole story is fishy to me."

"You're the Warner kid! I wondered what happened to you. I was assigned to the case."

"It's funny you say that. I was going to call you tomorrow to get information about what you saw at the scene."

"I can't divulge information on that, Joel. It's against regulations."

"Mr. Cox, I have agonized for years trying to figure out how they died. You are the only one with the information that could ease my mind and put this thing to rest, once and for all."

We talk for about an hour on what he saw that night. He looks at me, leans over and tells me, "Whatever you think happened that night did happen. I can't tell you anything about this, but if I do divulge any info about this, you will have to keep it to yourself. No one can know this. I have lived with the guilt over this for years. It's caused me physical problems. Ulcers, heart murmurs and chain smoking are just some of the symptoms I have lived with over the years because of this case. If I tell you what happened, you can't tell a soul. You deserve to know since it was your parents that died. I plan on retiring in a couple of weeks, or I wouldn't share a word of this with you."

I could tell that Larry has agonized with this for years. The guilt has eaten him up inside, especially since he has had no one to tell.

"Joel, I could lose my pension if this gets out. I only have a few more weeks till I retire. Do you understand where I am going with this?"

"I understand, what is said here tonight, stays here. I respect the fact that whatever information you have for me is of the utmost confidence. I will never break that trust."

"Bowman was drunk off his ass the night that accident happened. I had a report ready, sent it, and then found out the next day that I needed to *revise* it. He killed your parents, Joel. There is no other way to put it. I'm sorry you had to find out at this time, but the guilt is too much for me to handle. Every time I see that man on the news, or in a newspaper somewhere, I just want to vomit."

"Who made you revise your report? It just doesn't make sense."

"Well, the Mayor at the time, I am sure, wanted this swept under the rug. Bowman and the Mayor at the time were very close. The commissioner told my boss to have me change it, or heads would spin."

"You know this for a fact?"

"It's the way things work in that department, Joel. That is why if you tell anyone, both of our lives will be in danger."

I can see the load being lifted off Larry's back. Every word he speaks seems to make him more comfortable and me, more uncomfortable. It is hard to believe that he came here to question me about David and we end up talking about my parents' accident. My silent rage towards Bowman has come back. He is disgusting. How could someone do this and not have a conscience about it? If it were anyone else, they would have done a long stretch of hard time for that heinous a crime.

Larry says, "Thanks, Joel. I do feel better about telling you all of this information. I have wanted to tell you about this for some time, but never wanted to risk my job in doing so. I trust that you will keep your mouth shut."

"I will. By the way, what do you know about Sarah Munchak's disappearance? I saw articles about her while checking on my parent's accident."

"That is another story which I will not divulge any information. It was bad enough for me to tell you what I already have. I will tell you this, whatever you are thinking in regards to Bowman right now and the Munchak girl, well, you are probably right."

My mouth drops when I listen to this. I can't believe that no one from the press has picked up on any of this. A girl that worked for Bowman disappears and it gets zero publicity now. This is really pathetic.

"Thanks, Larry. Did you need to ask me any more questions about David?"

"No, I think I have everything I need. Just thought you might be able to shed some light as to why he would kill himself like that."

"I don't know. It was a normal conversation, but I had no idea he would do such a thing. It was the most disgusting thing I have ever seen."

"I bet. Well, if you can think of anything, call me."

"I do have a key to Ashley's apartment. I could go over there with you."

"I have to stop by the office and I'll meet you there in half an hour."

34

I feel like helping Larry as much as I can. I arrive early to Ashley's apartment. While waiting, I can't help but think that Jill and Ashley are now both gone. All the memories I have of the two of them are rambling through my mind very quickly. While I dive into my memories for a few moments, I hear a door slam. I look up and it's Larry, in front of my car with two cups of coffee.

"You know, kid, you really know how to make my day."

"Is this legal? Do you think I should call Ashley's mom to see if we have her permission to snoop a little?"

"It wouldn't hurt. There just might be something in that apartment which could lead us to her killer. David's note said that he had her killed, so if I can find just one clue, I will be happy."

I call Ashley's mom, knowing that she is probably a basket case. I hear her crying and sobbing. She tells me how sorry she is about what happened to Jill.

"How could anyone kill my Baby, Joel?"

"I don't know Mrs. Johnson, but I am here with a detective and we want to check out her apartment for any clues. Do you mind? Ash gave Jill and I a key a long time ago just in case of an emergency, but we would need your permission to enter her apartment."

"If you can find the bastard who killed her, do it! You are coming to her memorial service, aren't you?"

"I will definitely be there. When are you having it?"

"Saturday, I hope you can come, Joel. She loved you and Jill, so much."

"I'll be there, just give me directions."

After getting the time of the memorial and directions, I hang up with her. It's an awakening, knowing that the two women closest to me are gone. Larry looks at me and I tell him we can go inside. We enter her apartment. The shades are pulled down. A nasty stench is coming from within. When I cover my nose, Larry tells me to wait here. He pulls his gun and heads through the apartment very slowly. When he arrives to her bedroom, he turns slowly and tells me to call 911.

Larry does a little examination of her room. He carefully pulls her nightstand drawer open with his handkerchief covered hand. He finds a journal that Ashley kept. When he comes back out of the room, I ask if I can sit on her furniture. Larry tells me that I should put the journal in my car. He wants to go over it with me at my place.

"You can't say anything to anyone about that journal. That journal might take us right to the killer."

I take the journal and head toward my car. When I put the journal in the trunk, I hear the sirens coming. It was good getting out of that apartment. The stench started to make me light headed. After getting a few breaths of fresh air, I head back into the apartment, covering my nose and mouth with my hands. Larry tells me that I need to stay for a few moments in case there are any questions that may arise from the coroner's office. We keep the door of the apartment open to let some of the stench diminish.

He tells me to sit on her sofa while he handles the situation. Sirens are blaring now, but go dead when I hear the vehicles pull up into the parking lot. I hear footsteps running up the stairs and then four men walk in. Two look like cops and Larry talks to them. The other two look like they are taking Ashley's body out. One had a bag with a zipper on it, which must be a body bag.

My mind has kicked into overload. I can't believe all these people around me are dying. Thinking about all that has happened over the last week has been devastating. I have lost more people that are close to me than I have my entire life. My heart aches as I feel so alone now. Living is not important to me anymore. A life of a lonely existence is taking over. I have an *I don't care attitude* now.

An hour goes by after forensic examiners come in and go over her apartment with a fine tooth comb. Larry convinces me that they will not stay much longer. I just sit and wait. When I reach for a magazine on the end table next to me, I hear, "Don't touch that!"

Larry berates me, yelling at me to just sit still.

"Someone of importance could have left fingerprints on that magazine, Joel!"

I ask Larry if I could step outside and talk to him. When I take him downstairs I ask him in a whispering voice, "Can I go home, Larry? Come over after you're done here, so we can go over the journal."

"Sounds good, Joel. Do that while I finish up here. It shouldn't be too much longer."

While heading back to the apartment, my mobile phone rings.

"Nate! Where are you? I need to see you tonight!"

"What's going on, Joel?"

"It's about Ashley, Nate. I have some terrible news, buddy."

Nate starts to cry while talking to him. He tells me he has to hang up and the phone goes dead. I feel badly for him. I know he liked Ashley very much and wanted to know her more than he already did. I arrive home and see I have a message on my answering machine. It's Bill again, "Don't do the last one, Joel!"

The machine goes silent. These words are very disturbing. It's almost like he anticipates me killing someone else. I have no reason to, except for Bowman, but he isn't close to me. The only one left would be Nate, but there is no way I could kill Nate. He's my only friend left. I keep thinking about what Bill told me down in Carolina.

He said three people close to me would meet with a tragedy. I always thought that he meant death, but now I realize a tragedy could mean a number of things. While thinking about what he told me, I remember Ashley's journal being in my car. I go out to get it. I close the trunk of my car as I see Larry's car pull up next to mine.

"We need to talk, Joel."

After taking Larry back into the apartment, he sits down in the wingback. I ask Larry if he would like something to drink. He agrees to a beer. I pull two cans out of the fridge and he starts talking to me as I sit on the sofa.

"All of them left two minutes after you did, Joel. I snooped around and found out that Ashley had someone call her, leaving a message on her answering machine. It sounded like someone's voice that I have heard before. He said his name was

John. I know I have heard the voice before, Joel, and it sounds like a guy I busted a few years back. His name is Steve Cappo. He worked for the Chicago mob years ago. Steve just got out of prison about two years ago for assault. My guess is he did the hit on Ashley. I should have known David would have one of his clients do this."

"What do you mean, Larry?"

"A guy named Al Martelli runs the local mob here in Indianapolis. It all bases out of Chicago, but I remember back about five years when David Johns worked as Al's lawyer. David got him off, but I'm sure Al told David that he would do favors for him after he was acquitted of conspiring to kill someone, whom I can't remember. My guess is Steve works for Al and is the one that put the hit on Ashley."

"How would you know it is mob related, Larry?"

"I'm sorry to be so graphic, Joel, but Ashley was shot in the back of the head. It was a small caliber bullet. When the mob does a hit, they usually use a small caliber bullet, like a 22. That way there is little mess and not much splatter where it would show on clothing when they leave the scene. It was definitely a professional hit. Very clean. I have seen executions like this, which lead back to Steve, but we could never pin anything on him."

"Why do you think this Steve guy did it?"

"It just adds up. I thought about it on the way over here. Joel, the reason I am telling you this, is to see if you can remember anything about someone Ashley may have been associated with recently."

"Hmm, no one comes to mind, Larry. Wait! She did meet some guy over at Mike's Place about two weeks ago. Maybe it was him?"

"I'll check on that later. Let's take a look at that journal."

As I hand Larry the journal, I ask him to look through it and tell me if he notices anything interesting. With what has happened recently, I can't bear to read the intimate details of a good friend that has just passed. Larry is intently looking for any clues. He tells me that her last entry was last Friday at 3 p.m. I think back and know that was a couple of hours before Jill's showing.

He keeps reading and tells me that Jill and I are in the journal quite a bit. Larry reads excerpts from the journal that pertain to me. She wrote what a wonderful boyfriend I was to Jill. How she would pursue me if I weren't taken. Larry is getting a kick out of this, but it is just making me more depressed.

Larry finds something in the journal about Ashley and the guy she met at Mike's two weeks ago. She describes this man named 'John'. She described him as being tall, thin, clean shaven, dark hair and very Italian looking. Larry looks up from the journal and tells me that this may be Steve.

"He fits the description. It has to be him. Joel, if I bring a picture of this guy, do you think you could identify him? "

"Maybe Larry, Ashley played away games most of the time. She rarely brought guys over to her apartment. Ash almost always ended up at some guys place. My friend Nate was with her the day she disappeared. Maybe he could shed some light on the situation."

"Call him!"

I call Nate to invite him over. He lets it go straight to voicemail, I could tell from him not answering that he is still upset over losing Ashley. After leaving him a message, I look to Larry and ask him if he has found anything more. He shakes his head.

"I'm going back to the station. I will pick up a few photos and bring them back. Do you think if your friend Nate comes, you could keep him here until I get back?"

"I will certainly try, Larry."

When Larry leaves, I just sit on the sofa thinking about the craziness recently. I think of the devastation of losing Ashley. I hate to think this, but I am so numb to losing her. She was a great girl, but it's hard enough realizing that Jill is gone. Now I have to miss Ashley also?

I hear my phone ring, I answer knowing Nate is on the other end.

"Nate, I need you to come over right away."

"Why? Joel, I am so upset about Ashley being killed. I wonder if I am next. It seems that everyone around you is dying and I don't want to be next."

"Get over here. I didn't do anything to Ashley. David Johns had her killed. I have been helping out a detective on the case and he wants to speak to you."

"Is he there now? I can be there in about half and hour."

"He isn't here now, but will be within the hour. He stopped by the station to pick up a few photos of a guy he thinks might be the killer."

"I'll swing over shortly. I just need to get a shower."

"See you soon, bro."

I hang up and turn on the television hoping there might be a game on. Thinking about revenge and death are things that I need to put aside for right now. A nice baseball game might just get my mind off everything. I turn to the Reds versus the Cubs. It looks like a pretty good game. It's the bottom of the third and the score is 1-1.

While watching I lay out on the sofa just trying to rest my mind. I end up falling asleep.

35

I hear a loud knock on the door. When I get up and walk slowly to the door, I hear Nate yelling through the door that it is him. I answer the door. Nate walks in, and I look at him trying to understand that this is really my friend Nate. His face is pale. His big blue eyes are gone and replaced with dilated pupils, his dark eyes and pale face, with his skeletal overall appearance, makes me want to cry. I look at him wondering how long before he dies from this poison he keeps filling his body with.

"Joel, I can't sleep. I keep thinking that I am going to be knocked off next. Tell me you aren't going to kill me, Joel."

"Are you doing coke again, Nate? You always get paranoid when you do that crap. I would never think about killing you Nate."

"I think I am going out of my head. This is too much for me to handle, Joel."

Nate starts to cry. He sits in the middle of the family room floor, crosses his legs, puts his elbows on his thighs and grabs his chestnut brown hair in disbelief.

"Why would anyone kill Ashley?"

"I can't answer that, Nate. Some people in this world are just sick. You need to get a grip, Nate. That detective will be here shortly. You need to get that drugged up look off your face. You want some coffee? Maybe a shower would do you some good?"

"Brew some coffee. I'll go take a shower. Let me know when he gets here."

"I will. Just try and relax. Don't take any drugs before you see this cop. I need you to be cool when he arrives."

Nate tells me as he heads to the bathroom, "I ran out of everything this afternoon. I couldn't bring anything with me if I wanted to."

Nate walks to the bathroom and turns on the shower. I was thinking about all the yellow envelopes Larry saw when he was here earlier. I walk around the apartment and start cleaning up. I throw trash out and hide the envelopes in kitchen cupboards. Five minutes go by and I hear a knock on the door. When I open the door, Larry asks, "Is your friend here? I found a few pictures of Steve."

"He is here, taking a shower at the moment. Nate should be done shortly. Larry, I have wanted to ask you why you told me all the information about Bowman earlier. I don't understand why you would put your job at risk by telling me all that information."

"Joel, you would if you had seen the blood, murders, suicides and rapes that I have. Then you see a man like Bowman do something like what he did to your parents. Bowman has such a huge political following, with no one knowing what skeletons are hiding in his huge closet. When you told me you were the Warner kid, I had a lot of sympathy for you. I have two daughters, and I thought of them, if something like what you went through had happened to them, I couldn't fathom the thought of it."

"You are risking your job for me. I'll never betray your trust, but why are you doing this?"

"My job is to rid the streets of criminals. That is what I do. When I see politicians committing crime, doing the same crimes I am trying to rid the streets of, I get upset. There are so many things Bowman has done, and abused his power for years to cover them up, but I can't keep quiet anymore. I want to be heard and tell you and others, what kind of animal this guy has become."

"Do you think it's possible to get any of Bowman's previous crimes to stick?"

"The only way I could make anything stick to him, Joel, is if he confessed what he has done, vocally. A true confession, so to speak."

I think about what Larry just said. Nate walks into the room, and I introduce Nate to Larry. Nate immediately asks Larry why he wants to see him.

"I have some pictures I would like you to look at. There is a guy we are looking for. I'm hoping you will recognize him in one of these pictures."

Nate looks so much better after the shower, but I still can tell he is doing serious drugs. It wouldn't surprise me if he did a line while he was in my bathroom.

"I'll try and see if I can recognize any of them."

Nate looks over the pictures very carefully, studying each one. He comes across a picture where he recognizes the guy. Nate hands it over to Larry. When I see Larry's eyes light up, I know that Nate has picked Steve's photo.

"How do you know this guy, Nate?"

"He was walking up to Ashley's apartment the night she disappeared. I asked him what he was doing there, but he said he was from her work and needed to see Ashley for a minute. I went back inside Jill's apartment thinking that he might be a while, and fell asleep. I went back to Ashley's apartment about half an hour later when I woke up and she never answered. I just figured something important had happened at work and she left."

Larry looks at me, then at Nate.

"Would you testify in court that you saw this man the night Ashley disappeared?"

"Of course I would!"

Larry leaves and tells me on his way out that he will call me when he can locate Steve. I look at Nate. My eyes are wide open with shock.

"Why didn't you tell me about this sooner, Nate?"

"I didn't think anything of it. It didn't occur to me that I would know someone that would get whacked. I'm sorry, Joel. I miss Ashley a lot, but I never thought anyone would want to kill her. I still can't deal with it."

I look at Nate and think about what he has gone through. When I think about Ashley, I know she messed around with guys, but deep down I know she couldn't do anything to get herself killed. Nate looks at me, and then tells me he has to leave.

"I have a party to go to, Joel. You want to come?"

"Are you kidding me? I don't feel like getting high off my butt tonight, Nate."

"With losing Jill and now Ashley, maybe you should just go out and have a good time tonight and try to forget about everything."

"That's all right. I'm just going to go to Mike's for a couple hours, then come back home."

"Okay. I'll talk to ya."

Nate walks out in a rush. I close the door behind him and sit down on the sofa. It's about 11:30 p.m. now and I really don't feel like going to bed, or even watching television. A trip to Mike's just might put me in the mood to sleep.

When I walk into Mike's, I see a camera flash. I close my eyes trying to get rid of the blue dot I continuously see while blinking my eyes. Mike took my picture and he comes from behind the bar and says, "You're an Indianapolis celebrity now, Joel!"

"How's that?"

"You witnessed the biggest jerk in Indianapolis kill himself!"

I shake my head at Mike and sit at the bar. He puts a Blue Moon in front of me, saying it's on the house. While I take a sip, I see drunken Jim sitting a couple seats down looking at some pictures. I scoot down a seat hoping to get a glimpse of the pictures he's looking at.

"Jim, how are ya?"

"I'm good, how are you?"

He notices me glancing at the pictures and tells me, "Remember the chick that was here about a month ago?"

I think for a moment, hoping I can remember.

"Yeah, what was her name? I think it was Sherry, or Sheila."

"Sheila is right. I was hired by Sheila's husband to follow her. These are some of the pictures I got of her with that boy toy she had."

"Aren't you supposed to keep those pictures under wraps?"

"I already turned them over to the husband. I was just admiring my handiwork."

"They are pretty good shots. I can't believe she was that dumb, thinking she could get away with it."

Jim smiles and puts the pictures back in a yellow envelope. He glances up at the television behind the bar. My eyes follow his. When my eyes reach the television, I see Bowman on the screen and Jim says, "There's your favorite guy, Joel. It looks like you have another friend that killed himself today."

"That was no friend of mine, Jim. Actually, it was my ex-fiancées boss. I was just going to apologize for something I said at her showing last Friday."

"I heard about your fiancée, I'm sorry to hear about that, but I don't think her ex boss takes apologizes too well, Joel."

Jim giggles as he heads out the door. I call Mike over and ask him, "How did he know about what happened to me?"

"Everybody knows, Joel. It's been on television all day."

"I haven't had a chance to see much myself, except for my ugly mug, and then I turned the TV off."

"You are a legend, Joel. Even though you didn't kill him, you had the luxury of watching him die."

A few people in the bar overhear Mike and applaud, as I take another sip from my pint. I think about how sick this world is, a man dies a horrible death and people are happy about it. I killed him and I didn't feel any euphoria during, or after it happened. It was something I felt I had to do. If he were still living and I told police that David had killed Ashley, any officer that I told, would have laughed at me. I call it immediate justice.

I am still feeling a lot of remorse for killing David, yet I know deep down that he deserved it. My thoughts about killing Bowman are finished. It was bad enough killing Johns, but to kill Bowman might end up putting me in a loony bin. I want to take Bowman out so bad, but I don't want to see him dying on my television screen twenty years later, on some History Channel flashback. My conscience won't let me do it.

Mike puts another Blue Moon in front of me, as I take the last sip from my first pint. He tells me it's from a guy I don't even know, sitting at the other end of the bar. Mike tells me that the guy saw me on TV and wanted to give me a treat for my lousy day. I smile as Mike walks away. I wave to the man as I take my first sip.

While drinking from my beer I think of the comment I made to Jim about Sheila being dumb, thinking she wouldn't get caught. I guess the bad people do get caught some times. Maybe I just didn't think that happened too much. You constantly see how many people do bad things and get away with it. Newspapers, magazines and television always show you the politician, star or athlete getting away with a serious crime. That person may serve some time, but not the kind of time that a regular citizen would get if committing the same crime.

It's a lot like cutting out cancer. No matter how many bad people are locked up, there will always be more bad people out there waiting in line to take their place. It's so much easier to be bad than good. Being good takes too much effort, while being bad is almost effortless. It's no consolation that the ones that do well are the ones that end up the victim of someone acting on these bad impulses. I don't consider what I did to David, murder. I consider it cutting out a little bit of the cancer that has rotted our society.

I look up at the television and see Bowman on again. The anchorwoman is telling us that he will be appearing at a fund raiser Friday, for the Democratic Party here in town. She goes on to say that the tickets are one thousand dollars a piece. I glance back down at my beer, and I take another sip.

Mike comes over and says with a chuckle, that I should go to the fund raiser in hopes that Bowman might kill himself. I just look at Mike while he smiles and just shake my head, saying, "I'm out!"

I can't believe that there are people in this world whose only joy is the idea of someone famous or popular dying. My mind thinks of times where someone famous has passed, whether tragically or naturally. I can't think of anytime when I enjoyed someone dying. I always felt badly when an occurrence like that happened.

When I walk to the back door, Mike follows me out.

"Hey, Joel. I didn't mean any of that in there. I was just trying to make you laugh. I'm not going to lie to you, though. I am glad Johns died. He was a really bad character."

"I thought you were serious about those comments. They almost made me sick."

I smile at Mike as I start to walk away. He asks me to swing in tomorrow. I nod, knowing that I have nothing better to do with my time now. I might as well.

36

I wake up to the sound of my mobile phone ringing. When I check the caller ID, I see that Judy has made another attempt in trying to reach me. My thoughts are to let it go into voicemail, but for some reason I answer, wanting to talk to her. I hesitantly answer and hear her say, "Joel, Bill has told me that you are heading down a very dark path."

"I have been over this so much lately, Judy. I would have to agree with him."

"Why, Joel? I heard David Johns killed himself. You didn't have anything to do with that, would you?"

"I was there, but he wrote a note, and then killed himself. He wrote on the note that he had Ashley killed. I can't remember if I told you about her, but she was Jill's best friend. I apologized to him, and then he took his own life in gruesome fashion."

"You had nothing to do with this?"

"Judy, I didn't do it!"

I could tell she knows that I am lying. What have I become?

I have turned into a lying, killing and deceitful jerk. Of all the people that I have despised for being this way, I have now become one, just like them. It seems bad, but I don't feel any remorse. Has my conscience deserted me?

I keep talking to Judy and she asks me to come down, but I refuse. She is afraid that more bad things will happen to me. I thank her, but refuse, saying that I have some loose ends to tie up here. Judy tries one more time, saying that she is afraid for my life.

"I'm sorry, Judy, but I am doing fine. I have that forgiving spirit you were telling me about. I just don't see what could go wrong."

As she hangs up, she wishes me well. One lie right after another. What makes it worse is that I don't feel bad about the lies. It is one thing to lie to spare someone's feelings, but to lie for selfish reasons? Maybe I am too deep into this self-righteous attitude. I do know that my bitterness toward God may have started this cold delusion, but I have no remorse for what I've done at all.

I take a quick shower and then call around town and buy a ticket to Bowman's fund raiser on Friday. I succeed in finding a ticket. My day is one of reflection and self doubt. I spend hours sitting on the sofa wondering when my time to die might be. Bill has been so right as far as his prediction, it scares me. Maybe I should go to North Carolina and spend more time having Judy analyze me, but I just don't feel like being mentally butchered.

What if Bill ends up being right? He made it sound as though I might die a horrendous death, but who knows? It is possible that I might prove him wrong, but I won't be satisfied till Bowman blows his chance at the presidency. When I think about it for a little while, I call Judy back and tell her that I will be down there Saturday. She tells me that it is the right thing to do and that she is expecting me. We hang up when she finishes the conversation by saying, "Joel, just stay out of trouble till then."

I turn on the television trying to find something on that will occupy my mind. There must be something on to take my mind off of this whirlwind of self doubt I have. While flipping through channels, I hear a loud bang on the door. I go to answer and I see it's Larry.

"Joel, open up, I have some good news!"

When I open the door Larry walks in and it seems as though he is in a good mood.

"We picked up Steve Campo last night. He made all sorts of excuses, but if your friend Nate can testify in court that he saw him at Ashley's, then we may have him locked away for a long time. We found a 22 pistol on him and are running it through ballistics right now as we speak."

"Man, that sounds too good to be true."

"What's weird though, Joel, he almost sounds believable?"

"He's just a good liar. That's all it is. How many years has he been doing this?"

"You make a good point, Joel, but I have seen criminals like him for years, lie about alibis constantly, but for some reason he was somewhat convincing. I guess we'll know for sure when the ballistics tests are done against the gun and the slug we removed from Ashley."

His comments remind me that I need to call Ashley's mom and find out when the funeral for Ashley is taking place. I may have to postpone my trip to North Carolina, so I can go. Ashley was a dear friend and I know I wouldn't be able to forgive myself if I didn't go.

Larry tells me that he wanted to stop by and let me know that he found Steve, and then he leaves. I go back to my sofa, lie down and fall asleep.

I wake back up hours later and see that it is now 9:00 p.m. Mike is expecting me at his place tonight, so I throw some jeans on and a t-shirt, hoping that my stay there won't be long. When I arrive, I see that only two people are sitting at the bar. I hear Led Zeppelin's *Since I've Been Loving You* playing softly throughout the bar. What a perfect song for a bluesy kind of day. I sit at the bar, Mike comes up to me from behind the bar and I tell him, "It seems like your business is picking up, Mike."

"Funny, Joel, real funny."

It is so quiet in here, I can hear myself think. Mike asks me, "How are you doing? Did this suicide thing get to you?"

"Not as badly as you might think, Mike."

He keeps talking to me, trying to cheer me up. His bad jokes and light conversation is nice, but I keep thinking about my own mortality. While talking and listening to Mike, I feel a need to call Bill. A call to him might clear my mind a bit, but for now, a good night out talking to Mike and having a few, might be what I need.

Hours go by, watching TV, talking to strangers that sit next to me, and listening to Mike's anecdotes. It was a refreshing night, not dealing with a drugged up friend, or anybody dying. Before I realize it, Mike is announcing last call. I never have been here for last call and I can't believe the night has to end. I enjoyed meeting new people, and for the first time since Jill's death, enjoyed living again.

It was good pushing all my mental anguish aside for a night and enjoying life. Mike asks me if I want another, but I just shake my head, throw some bills on the bar, and head out. When I get home, I go straight to bed and fall immediately to sleep.

37

It's Thursday morning, I wake up at 9:00 a.m. hoping to call Ashley's mom to find out when the funeral is taking place. When I call, it goes straight to the answering machine. I leave a message for her to call me and let me know what time I should be in Columbus. As soon as I hang up, I call Bill. His phone rings and rings. I'm unable to leave a message. It seems he doesn't have an answering machine.

I sit on the sofa, very nervous and edgy. When I see it's now 9:30, I head out to Café Indy for some coffee and to read the newspaper. Upon arrival at the coffee shop, I see a newspaper on one of the tables. Headlines on today's issue reads, *The Truth About David Johns,* I read a few lines, just to see if any new dirt has been written about him. I take the paper with me to the counter and order a cup of my Jamaica Blue Mountain coffee. I throw a couple bucks on the counter as I pick up my cup, still reading.

When I sit down, I see that David Johns was into defending guys that were part of organized crime. He spent time trying to separate his name from it, but it seemed to follow him, even after his death. People didn't talk about it much. It seemed to be rumors more than anything factual. I guess that's why Larry probably thought this Steve Campo guy rubbed Ashley out. He knew Steve had been associated with David in the past and just put two and two together.

I put the paper down and just look around this establishment. Maybe finding someone I know, just to say *hi*. While taking a sip from my coffee, my phone rings. I answer, "Larry, what's up?"

"The test came back, Joel. Ashley's slug didn't come from Campo's gun."

"Could he have used another gun to kill her?"

"We're checking into it, but don't have a thing yet."

"I'm at Café Indy, want to join me? I have a couple questions about David Johns and the mob. I was reading the paper. It caught my eye that he defended a couple of these guys. Did he defend Steve at all?"

"I guess I could join you, things here are stagnate until we here back from the investigators checking out Steve's gun collection. I'll tell you about David and Steve when I get there."

"Okay, I'll wait for you, see you soon. Bye."

I hang up and call Judy to let her know I won't be coming down Saturday. She answers, "Joel, tell me you are coming?"

"I am, but I forgot that I promised Ashley's mom I would travel to Columbus for Ashley's funeral."

"Don't break your promise, Joel. I cancelled some lectures this coming week, so I could spend some time making you feel better about yourself."

"I appreciate it, Judy. I will be there Tuesday. I think the funeral is Monday, but I haven't heard for sure. If the day changes, I will call and let you know."

"It's good hearing from you, Joel. Take care."

I hang up with her, calling Nate, hoping he has heard any details about the funeral. I call Nate and he answers the phone and half asleep he says, "It better be important, Joel."

"Have you heard anything about when Ashley's funeral is taking place?"

"Try the obituaries moron! I'm going back to bed, call me later, Joel."

I smile thinking that I must have missed out on a good time last night. There is no way I was going to that party. I can't party like that. It hurts my body to much the next day to do it anymore. I'm not in college. When I think about how bad Nate must be hurting, I chuckle some more. I glance up at the clock above the counter and see that it has been almost half an hour since talking to Larry.

Patiently waiting, I go to the counter and order another cup of coffee. While paying for it, I hear Larry shout my name from across the room. I turn and see him walking toward me. I point to the table I was sitting at and he follows the tip of my finger to the empty table, where a newspaper and empty cup sit. He sits down at the table as I pay for the cup and head that way.

When I sit down, Larry asks me a couple questions.

"We can't find anything on Steve, Joel."

"Did you see if David Johns had a 22 stored somewhere?"

"I thought about it, but if he had one, he wouldn't be dumb enough to hide it in an obvious place."

"Larry, he was the most arrogant man I have ever known. He would be that stupid, thinking that he couldn't be touched because of who he was."

"You make a good point. I could check his office today, just in case."

"I don't think it could hurt, Larry."

We talk for a few minutes about the case. He thanks me for my help and insight. When he leaves the coffee shop, I leave the café myself, heading home to do laundry.

When I get home I put a load of laundry in the washing machine and clean my apartment. While cleaning, I decide to turn on some music. I turn my phone off not wanting to be disturbed. A few moments to myself is all I require in getting through another emotional day. Nothing from the outside world will penetrate this apartment. All the murder and chaos in my life needs to leave.

Cleaning this apartment is a bad chore, but is done now. It took about an hour to vacuum, clean the counters and polish the wood furniture. I sit in my wingback chair and admire my work for a moment. Music fills the room and I am taken by it. I put some Robert Johnson in the stereo, it seemed perfect for the mood I am in. Blues always seems to make me feel better when I hear it. The words remind me that someone has suffered as much, if not more than I have.

I close my eyes and feel the words sooth my soul. A pathetic feeling, for someone that has lost a few people in his life, has a friend doing drugs, and a lonely existence ahead of him. A tiny smile comes to my face when I think of everything I have been through. If I could just write the words down, with everything that has happened, I could have a couple hundred songs written.

While Robert keeps singing, I think of how precious life is. Mike's last night opened my senses a little bit as to how much I should embrace life. New people I get to meet, music I enjoy because it makes me feel emotion, my senses of touch, taste, feel and smell being stimulated by many things. The smell outside after a driving rain on a spring day, the taste of coffee after brewing, touching the silky skin of the woman you love. Although lately it has been horrible, I remember times where I felt wonderful. When something good happened to Jill, I felt like I was going through what she felt, as though it were happening to me.

These things I feel about life are just a few of the ones rambling through my mind. Life is too short. It is worth living, living a full and fulfilling life is what one makes of it. I haven't made much of mine lately, except for getting revenge on those that have taken people close to me. No disrespect here, but the people that were close to me are now all dead. What gratification did I really get when I killed David Johns? He has a wife that is now a widow, and his kids will never know him. David's life was full of pros and cons, but deep down I know I did the right thing.

My problem now is deciding whether I should go to the banquet and ruin Bowman's chances at the presidency. Munchak and my parents are gone, but I feel I should just ruin his chances, not take him out. It makes no sense to kill him, but if I could make him bow out with a sense of honor. I think that would make me feel better.

I sit, slouched in the chair, with my head half way down the back of the chair. I feel so lazy that I can't even slide myself back up. I need to get up and go to the bathroom, but a moment like this is what I have longed for since Jill died, a moment where I don't have to deal with the outside world. I am able to isolate myself from my thoughts.

Mother Nature finally wins and I head to the bathroom. My moment of bliss has been set aside. When I get done, listening to music, turning on the television and ordering a pizza sounds like a good way to spend the rest of the day, away from the world. The pizza man is the only one I plan to talk to today, and that is just fine with me.

38

It's Friday morning and I've just hauled myself out of bed. My nerves start, as I debate within myself whether I attend the fund raiser. Revenge appeals to me, but I am desperately trying to put the settling of any more scores behind me. I'm worried about what will happen in the future, if I don't do anything to Bowman now. Will I be happy in the future if he does do something bad, knowing that I could have changed the outcome before it happens?

Debate seems to have ruled my psyche for the last couple of days. I liked Judy's advice about concentrating on making my life better and not dwelling on anger and rage. It sounded like a great idea until David told me he had Ashley killed. I keep wondering if anyone else would have done the same thing. It is almost impossible to guess, let alone have a resounding *yes*.

I feel like going. After all, I did buy a ticket. Although I don't have a date, I'm sure I will meet some interesting people tonight. One thousand bucks for dinner and a speech from a man I can't stand. It sounds like I might be spending a night at the threshold of hell.

My coffee for the morning is brewing as I eat cold pizza out of the box, from last night. I feel a sense of hope overtake my soul, a feeling that is hard to describe. I want to start my life anew. I want to join a gym and get into shape, buy a ragtop and travel the country, and maybe visit the lonely and less fortunate in area hospitals. I need to connect with a purpose in my life again.

I turn on my mobile phone and see that I have a voicemail. It is a call from Ashley's mother. Her message says that she wants me to come Saturday to visit. She says Ashley's funeral will be Monday, but that the family is receiving friends Saturday and Sunday at the funeral home.

My hatred of funeral homes arise once again, but knowing it's for Ash, makes me believe I can handle it. I can't stand funeral homes, but hospitals are even worse. The smell of death reeks throughout the halls, with an undertone of medicine following it. It is a smell that makes you glad to be alive, hoping you never have to go there for any reason except to visit.

The day is uneventful as I get clothes ready for the fund raiser. I am so glad that I bought this tuxedo a few years back, knowing that it would come in handy sometime. The time is now 3:00 p.m. and I need to be at the hotel by 6:30 p.m. My tux looks great, as I try it on for the first time in ages. It is a penguin affair tonight. A black tie affair is what everyone else calls it, but I always imagine these functions, a bunch of middle aged men in tuxes drinking martinis.

For me to make an appearance at this get together tonight, may cost Bowman his chance at the presidency, but I maybe can have fun in the process. I take a shower, shave and get dressed before 5:00 p.m. It is time to make my way downtown. It will only take me fifteen minutes by car. When I arrive at the hotel,

I am greeted at the entrance to the banquet hall, by several people from the Democratic Party.

I take my assigned seat at one of the huge round tables, which seats ten people. It is hard to believe the kind of people that show up for something like this. People that I have only seen on the news, or on an entertainment show. Actors, athletes and politicians are everywhere I look. It surprises me when a couple Colts players come over and introduce themselves. We spend half an hour talking about the upcoming football season, politics, and of all things, the weather. It is July now and the weather is ridiculously sunny. We have had something like twenty five days straight, without a drop of rain.

Maybe this is just what I needed. I have met at least ten people tonight, and they all seem to be very intelligent. It is so nice having a conversation with a group of smart individuals. My thoughts are interrupted by the applause as Senator Bowman walks in the room. He smiles and greets people as he works the room. His hand reaches for mine and as I shake it, our eyes meet. Bowman's smile turns to a frown.

He seems uncomfortable now. Bowman must know who I am. Does the memory of my parents run through his mind? Why did his smile leave as soon as I shook his hand? He must know something about me, but what? He leaves me and shakes the hands of many others while keeping the smile pasted in place. Since I came here intending to cause Bowman to confess his wrong doings, maybe he can feel my vibe.

As he takes his seat, I can see him sweating and pulling the collar of his shirt as though his nerves are getting to him. Sweat beads on his forehead and drips slowly down his face. I can see his wife lean over and ask him, "What's the problem?" I am not a lip reader, but his wife's lips are easy to read, even from this distance. My thoughts are of Bowman smothered under a blanket of guilt for what he has done in the past.

My curiosity hits me. If I am able to stir up all this guilt, maybe he will confess everything without me having to force his hand. We eat and drink, as conversations continue all around me. The people at my table are very interesting. A couple CEO's, a bank president, a self employed millionaire, and their wives make up the mix. A woman that works for the Democratic Party here in town sits next to me. She is interesting, but too much of a political mind for my taste. Her passion for her beliefs is very admirable, but she has an over the top overzealous quality about her.

I see that Bowman keeps glancing over at my table. He still looks scared and nervous. Maybe he will confess by himself tonight. We all get up from our tables and mingle. When I turn to my left, I find myself face to face with Senator Bowman. He grimaces and shakes my hand.

"I checked the attendees for tonight's fund raiser. I recognized your name on the guest list. Do you know where I am headed with this?"

"Do you mean, am I the son of the parents that were killed, in the accident you were involved in about ten years ago? Yes, that would be me."

"I am so sorry about what happened that night."

"Sorry, Mr. Bowman? My parents were murdered! I was eighteen at the time. Do you realize how hard that has been for me?"

Bowman has a look of sorrow on his face. His eyes are bloodshot and his face is full of emotion.

"I've done some things in my past Joel that I am ashamed of and regret. Tonight may cost me the presidency. My conscience has been bothering me about that night long ago, especially coming face to face with you. I think about the pain that you have been through and what it must have been like without your parents."

"Do you think of Sarah Munchak also?"

A sense of rage can be seen in Bowman's eyes. He turns away from me, hoping he doesn't lose his cool. Bowman walks away and resumes shaking hands and flashing that fake smile of his. He glances back at me with a cold stare.

An announcement is made that a few words will be spoken by Senator Bowman. We take our seats and Bowman heads toward the podium. He has a somber look to him. His voice cracks as he starts speaking.

"I want to thank all of you for coming tonight. I have seen many new faces tonight as well as old ones. Your help getting me nominated has been one of dedication and perseverance, of which I thank you. My heart is very heavy tonight. I have many thoughts in my mind, but the most predominant is that my political career must end tonight."

Everyone looks at each other in amazement. I haven't even tried to get him to confess. This is all Senator Bowman's doing.

"I have many skeletons in my closet which force me to stop my pursuit in the next Presidential election. My next wish is to speak to the authorities in regards to the Sarah Munchak disappearance."

Bowman looks directly at me. His eyes are full of tears. People in the crowd have confused looks on their faces. People that have spent countless hours supporting a man hear him bear his soul to the world and are confused by this drastic turnaround in his political aspirations.

"There is one gentleman here that is long overdue and deserves to know the truth. I was drunk when I hit your parent's car, Joel. I am so sorry that I had people cover this up for years."

His eyes still gaze out into the crowd as he bears his soul. He uses these final moments closing his speech. Security that was earlier used for defending Bowman is in place to detain him.

My mind is in shock. I keep wondering if somehow I made him do this, just the idea of Bowman confessing, not only has shocked me, but everyone else in the room. I was determined to have Bowman confess, but no one here ever guessed that Bowman would unleash this bottled up guilt he had.

Bowman slowly walks off the mini stage into the arms of security. Handcuffs are put on the man who just sacrificed the presidency for honor. I must say, I am impressed. My parents are gone, but I know if they were alive they would also be impressed also. I don't know how Sarah Munchak's parents will deal with the news of their daughter, but I am sure they will finally have some peace.

The lights are turned up and I can see many people in the room visibly upset. We are directed to leave the hotel while the police take Senator Bowman in for questioning. I start to head home and listen to the news on the radio. It is full of stories about how crooked and bad Bowman has been. People keep talking about him as though they suspected he was like that all along. These are many of the same people that were ready to vote for him in the upcoming Presidential election.

I turn off the radio. My mental disgust can't take anymore. I believe that Bowman should serve time for what he has done, but I do respect him more since his confession. He does have a badge of honor now. It's small, but it is a badge nonetheless. When I arrive home, I lie down on the sofa and turn on the television. I turn on national news and see the different angles of the story being covered.

After a few hours of watching the news, I head to bed, but not after realizing a huge weight being lifted off my back. Justice has finally been done. Finally my Jill, Ashley, mom and dad, can rest in peace. A life of happiness and prosperity awaits me tomorrow.

39

It's Saturday morning. I start this day like any other Saturday. Before I go to the Café Indy, I take a shower, get dressed and hurry out the door. While driving to the café, I hear the news come on the radio, *"Senator Bowman hung himself late last night."*

I pull the car off the road and park in the McDonalds parking lot. I concentrate on every word spoken.

"After telling police where they could find Sarah Munchak. He was placed in a holding cell, where he hung himself with a belt. Indianapolis Police stated that Bowman gave a full confession of killing Miss Munchak before he hung himself."

I look at the radio, thinking that the reporter will say it is some sort of sick joke. It sickens me to think Bowman felt so guilty that he took his own life. When I think of how much his conscience must have overwhelmed him last night, I guess I understand his actions. I know I wasn't very forgiving of him, but it had given me a certain release, emotionally.

When I reach the counter at Café Indy, my order is placed. I pay for my coffee and a newspaper and move to a nearby table. I spread out the newspaper. The front page headlines are in lettering that I have never seen before. *Bowman Dead* covered the top half of the newspaper. I read the article about Bowman confessing to the police about sexual misconduct, murder, rape and vehicular homicide. My parent's accident is briefly mentioned.

The article goes on to say that Bowman gave the exact location where Sarah Munchak's bones are hidden. A map was drawn for police to find her. I look up from the paper and see CNN headlines mention that Sarah Munchak's bones have been found. I look at the television, but no sound is coming out of it, so I try to read the lips of the news anchor again. It looks as though Sarah was found just two hours after Bowman hung himself.

When I finish my coffee, I order another cup, fold the paper and leave. I drive home thinking about the craziness this city has witnessed for the last two weeks. I also ponder that maybe I helped him think of what he did in his past. Did I do this subconsciously with Bowman hanging himself? My parking lot is somewhat empty when I pull in. I park my car next to Nate's. He must be here waiting for me to get back. I grab my head with both hands wondering if I am going mad. I don't know if my power is more than what I originally thought with Bowman killing himself. I have no idea if I had anything to do with it.

I see him in his car with the driver side seat tilted all the way back. Nate must not have had much sleep. When I tap on the driver side window, he jumps up in amazement. I shake my head and walk toward the front door of my apartment. Nate follows right behind.

Nate follows me in and slams the door behind him. He asks me how my night went and smiles. His smile slowly turns to a frown when I tell him that I couldn't believe Bowman killed himself.

"He did? I hear last night that he gave himself up, but didn't hear about him killing himself."

"Well, Nate, you might want to take a look at the TV news."

Nate kind of blows me off when I turn to see him, snooping around my kitchen.

"What are you looking for, Nate?"

"Nothing in particular. A glass maybe, for some water."

After pouring himself a glass of water. I see his hand shake as he puts the glass to his lips. His lips quiver as he takes the first sip.

"Are you okay, Nate?"

"Joel, I need your help. I have a lot of debt to cover. My drug habit got worse and I need your help. I owe about sixty grand."

"Wait here. I'm going to the restroom first, then we'll talk."

While in the bathroom, I hear cupboard doors slam. I realize that Nate might be snooping for the yellow envelopes. When I get back I see that Nate has found the envelopes and placed them on the counter. He asks me, "Is this all you have, Joel? I remember sending twelve of these, but I can only find five of them. Where are the others, Joel?"

I try to answer Nate, but am interrupted by my mobile phone ringing. It's Ashley's mom, wanting to know when I plan on coming. When I tell her that I'm leaving in about an hour, I glance over at Nate and see the rage building inside him. He shakes with fury. I turn to look out the window and finish my conversation with Ashley's mom. I hang up the phone and I turn towards Nate. I feel a sharp cold feeling crawling up my back.

I keep reaching behind my back hoping to find out what is

happening to me. Nate is about a foot away from me. When I look him in the eyes, he tells me.

"I asked you so many times to help me, Joel."

Tears flow from his eyes. At this moment I realize I have been stabbed. The cold steel rubs against my bones and I start to chill. I fall to the ground on my knees.

"Nate, I forgive you, please just take the knife out. My body is turning cold."

I look at Nate, but can only see an image of him. It's like watching an old TV with snow on it, but still being able to see the images behind it. The pain is excruciating as I lie on the ground, while Nate stands there, not knowing what to do.

I feel the blood leave the hole in my back and warm my skin as it drips to the floor. At this point I realize that my breath is getting shorter. I feel somewhat paralyzed as I hear the cupboards open, and slam shut. Nate is so high right now. I don't think he will remember in a few hours that he stabbed me.

My thoughts are so clear right now that I ask God to forgive me. Tears start to stream down my face. I'm not afraid of dying, just upset that I couldn't live the rest of my life the way I should have. Nate comes up to me and tells me he needs money now.

"I would have given it to you if you, Nate."

"You're lying, Joel. You would never have given me the money."

Tears fall from my face like rain, and I grab enough breath to tell him, "I'm sorry, I brought this out of you, Nate. I never thought some harmless fun would cause so much damage. I'm so sorry, Nate. Please forgive me."

As a loud cry comes from Nate, he tells me, "I'm sorry, Joel. I haven't been that good of a friend."

I take one last glance at Nate, wondering what could have possessed him to do such a thing. As I close my eyes to soak up the pain he tells me, "You have the power to kill me, Joel. Why don't you? I feel so awful."

I speak one more time before I faint.

"There's been too much killing, Nate. I can't kill anymore. I won't let me. Just know that I forgive you."

He packs up the envelopes, removes the knife from my back, wipes off the handle and leaves the apartment. Tears fall faster as I feel my lungs fill with blood. I never thought death would be this painless. I start to pray, hoping that forgiveness is within my reach. I close my eyes and fall asleep.

Printed in the United States
89244LV00002B/49-51/A